THE ROURKE CHRONICLES
VOLUME I
EVERYMAN

Books in The Survivalist Series by Jerry Ahern

#1: Total War
#2: The Nightmare Begins
#3: The Quest
#4: The Doomsayer
#5: The Web
#6: The Savage Horde
#7: The Prophet
#8: The End is Coming
#9: Earth Fire
#10: The Awakening
#11: The Reprisal
#12: The Rebellion
#13: Pursuit
#14: The Terror
#15: Overlord

Mid-Wake
#16: The Arsenal
#17: The Ordeal
#18: The Struggle
#19: Final Rain
#20: Firestorm
#21: To End All War
The Legend
#22: Brutal Conquest
#23: Call To Battle
#24: Blood Assassins
#25: War Mountain
#26: Countdown
#27: Death Watch

Books in The Survivalist Series by
Jerry Ahern, Sharon Ahern and Bob Anderson
#30: The Inheritors of the Earth
#31: Earth Shine
#32: The Quisling Covenant
The Shades of Love (Short Story)
Once Upon a Time (Short Story)
Light Dreams (Short Story)

Books by Bob Anderson
Sarge, What Now?
Anderson's Rules
Grandfather Speaks

TAC Leader Series
#1 What Honor Requires
#2 Night Hawks
#3 Retribution

THE ROURKE CHRONICLES

VOLUME I

EVERYMAN

The story of **THE SURVIVALIST**, John Thomas Rourke, from my perspective—Paul Rubenstein.

With assistance from Jerry Ahern, Sharon Ahern and Bob Anderson, an authorized companion series for Jerry Ahern's **THE SURVIVALIST**.

Jerry Ahern, Sharon Ahern and Bob Anderson

SPEAKING VOLUMES, LLC
NAPLES, FLORIDA
2014

THE ROURKE CHRONICLES
VOL I: EVERYMAN

Creative research provided by Steve Servello. Editing assistance provided by Pamela Anderson. On Sheep, Wolves, and Sheepdogs, copyright Dave Grossman. Permission to use. Parable of the Pencil Maker. Public domain.

ISBN 978-1-62815-208-1

For more exciting
Books, eBooks, Audiobooks and more visit us at
www.speakingvolumes.us

DEDICATION

To Jerry and Sharon's old friend Steve Fishman, and to Steve Servello. Steve Servello's knowledge of the Rourke adventures cast him as my shortstop, my guide, my conscience; without him this book would not have been possible. For our readers here is a new perspective on the story.

Remember to Plan Ahead!

FOREWORD

On behalf of Jerry's entire estate, I would like to thank Paul Rubenstein for his kind words regarding Jerry and his efforts in documenting the earlier exploits of John Rourke. Yes, Jerry's books did lean heavily into the action-adventure genre, but where else would stories of the Rourke family escapades dwell? One might argue that this is our history, the history of our planet from the day things changed forever. But, if Jerry had written a history book it probably would never have been published; or, if it had, would have been read by only a few. However, by relying on a readership craving stories of heroic deeds, romance, and epic battles, Jerry's books of the Rourke exploits found their way into millions of homes all across the world.

Jerry spent many an evening sitting out on John Rourke's patio with his taping device and a gazillion questions. They would sit, smoke, and sip some Seagram's Seven. Sometimes Emma would join them for a while, curious about some of the earlier times that she had missed with John. Mostly though, they sat alone, John reminiscing as they both looked up at the stars.

We are certain that Paul's efforts to fill in the gaps in their family history have been a long, arduous affair and a self-reflective journey like no other. Through fiction, the Rourkes and Rubensteins became legends; through Paul's historical retelling, they have become America's heroes.

Sharon Ahern

INTRODUCTION

My name is Paul Rubenstein. With very few exceptions, I have known John Rourke longer than any person alive today, those exceptions of course being the other members of the Rourke family I mentioned. There are three questions I get all of the time; each is related to the others.

How long have I known John Rourke?

How did we first meet?

What kind of a man is he really?

To answer any of them, it is necessary to answer all of them, and I believe I am in a unique position to do so. I don't know that I have ever known or ever will know all there is to know about John Rourke.

I have heard the Rourke family referred to as "Heroes of Mankind," and John Thomas Rourke as "the chief among that illustrious pantheon." Legends and myths have abounded about our adventures, our battles, our very lives. Sometimes, I laugh at the stories. You see, I was there in the beginning. I was there living those adventures, those battles.

I have been called many things, but I am just a man; even though I wasn't much of one in the beginning, I have to admit. It was a journey to discover "who" I am today. But even today, I remain first of all just a man. We did not set out to become "Heroes of Mankind." We were simply trying to survive—survive the end of our world, all that we knew, the end of all of our dreams—near total devastation.

John's life had always been filled with danger. I've been asked, "Did John Thomas Rourke choose it or did it choose him?" Personally, I don't think it really matters; it was what it was. He, and we, faced every challenge; we saw every disaster through. The end of our world came and went and the world of our youth vanished.

Honestly, I don't know how many books have been written about the exploits of John Thomas Rourke and what has become known as his family. All of what has been presented has elements of the truth; but some have been written as action stories, some as historical accounts. In fact, the latter is my reason for this effort. Honestly, I have given up trying to count the number of times this book has been started.

It actually began shortly after our initial meeting, a meeting I will never forget. In that instant, I went from a quiet journalist and semi-practicing Jewish boy to the man I have become; I was thrust into a world I never conceived of. Had it not been for John, I would have never survived; our world did not.

These accounts and my feeble attempts have two purposes. One is to tell some stories that have not been recounted before or to give details that have been forgotten, misplaced, or simply never known because no one asked us. The second is to finish what I started so many years ago.

That first evening when John and I had finally rested, I took out a notebook and started reflecting on what had happened to us. That notebook disappeared a few days later after a gunfight and a wild motorcycle ride. Over the years, I lost many notebooks, stacks of notes, and hours of recordings. Now, today in this world, I will have to rely on factual accounts that have been written, insights that I and I alone had, and details from other members of our family.

Let me begin with some details before John and I met. No, I had never heard of him; in fact, I had no idea he existed. Actually, I had no idea people like him existed except in the pages of history and action-adventure novels and movies. Over our many adventures, I have met several other men with his qualities as well as a few women. Admittedly though, John is somewhat unique.

As I write this, I have two immediate thoughts. First, I don't believe in any actual conversation with him I have ever called him anything but John or John Rourke. In our conversations, I don't believe I have ever used his full name, the name that most people today refer to him by... John Thomas Rourke.

My second thought is about you the reader, what you might be able to gain and how you might be able to benefit from my story. John could not have found rawer clay to work with than me. There was an old television show before the

Night of the War about a family; their son was also a writer. His name was Richie. My life before John Rourke was like that television show; I truly lived in happier days.

As often happens, through no fault of my own, I was thrust into a world I didn't understand and was not equipped to deal with. There are only six of us alive today who were alive before they closed the door on the passenger plane that John and I boarded. When the attack came, our pilots were incapacitated by the blast; John was forced to try to land the plane. Several survived the crash landing.

As I said, there have literally been volumes, possibly even libraries, dedicated to John Rourke and, if I may call them exploits—the exploits of our family. Yes, it is our family. I have been his friend, his student, his "faithful Jewish sidekick," and now I am proud to say I am his son-in-law, married to his daughter Annie. This marriage fulfilled my life, my soul, and my heart; it was an honor akin to being John's sidekick, but better.

For me personally, our earlier adventures were the most difficult. I knew little of value and was in a constant training mode. Luckily, I had a good teacher. I will jump ahead of this story to help you understand John and the way the family has learned to operate. Each of us had to grow into being strong and unique individuals; many share dynamic skills. John has never been one to unnecessarily or inappropriately enforce his will on us. There are, however, three specific exceptions that John Rourke will enforce his reality on without hesitation.

If what is about to occur involves blood, if what is about to occur involves fire or, if what is about to occur involves forever, John would assume the role of leader—without hesitation—usually leaving very little room for the further negotiation. During those times, John succeeded in cutting through my fears. The fact was I didn't know what to do and was scared of failing.

Even when struggling with his feelings for Natalia, he was able to assess with certainty the differences between what "felt good" and doing the "right thing." He remained a father to his children and a dedicated husband to Sarah. John struggled with loving his family and finding something unexpected in Natalia. In the end, life happened with John and, for that matter, to me. Our lives today are not what we started out in search of.

Because of the sheer amount of written material associated with this story, I will use one of the most faithful accounts to supplement my efforts. I never met the author, but I understand he claimed to have known John Rourke and the history of his exploits better than anyone else. All I can say is the author's first name was Jerry. The exploits of the Rourke family had taken place by the time Jerry and John Thomas Rourke met. His chronicling of those exploits was based on interviews he had conducted with John during those sixteen years of relative peace.

John confirmed to me that Jerry's efforts were the most accurate, if a little bit action-oriented. However, in fairness to Jerry, John Rourke personified action in everything he did. I personally feel Jerry's accounts were the most accurate; and since Jerry has passed away, I have been in contact with Jerry's estate and the family has given permission for this effort. They had only one stipulation—I was not to use Jerry's full name. Their comment was, "Anyone who has read his books will know Jerry."

Initially, I thought to change the typeface when I quoted directly from his works. I believed that would make it easier for me and for the reader to keep track of what's happening and who is telling it, while giving Jerry credit for his original works. Unfortunately, I was mistaken. It became far more laborious than functional.

I can tell you however, that Jerry's family has reviewed this work and it truly is an authorized version of the events as related by Jerry in his original works; and, on the basis of my memory of events—not a lame attempt at plagiarism.

Let me take you back to the days before that plane left Canada and tell you a story you are probably familiar with, but definitely not from this perspective.

PART I

THE DAY THE TOTAL WAR BEGAN

CHAPTER ONE

My name is Paul, Paul Rubenstein. When I landed at the Calgary International Airport, I remember thinking, "At least there are no polar bears here." I wasn't the least concerned about the end of the world and the start of a war. To say I was politically naïve, not only from the point of current events, but to even have a political stand was an understatement. I lived in the moment; my problems were normal stuff like work. Plus, I had overly protective parents that I thought were still locked in the problems Jews in Europe had been dealt before the last major war. To me all of that was history, the kind you watch in old black and white movies or horrors you read about.

I was auditioning for a position as a junior editor; something even my girlfriend Ruth Bixon was not aware of. I had been trapped into what was "a project that really should be considered an adventure" by my soon-to-be boss, I hoped, Derek Vicenza—owner and editor of the *North Country* magazine. *North Country* was a full color publication that covered a variety of activities and venues from the "great outdoors" to gourmet cooking (albeit with moose and elk) and fashion statements (usually dealing with animal furs and whale bone).

I was to roam about the great Canadian prairie, perhaps venture a bit into the nearby foothills of the Rockies and discover angles for stories for *North Country* magazine. Vicenza had told me, "I like you kid; I'd really like to see what you can do for us. You're a good writer, as demonstrated by your string book, but we have a different feel and clientele. I want to see if you can make the transition to our kind of magazine. Alberta is the place for you to make the connection, and I'm willing to finance a couple of weeks to see what you can do."

I was pretty sure a polar bear would have to have come down from the Arctic Circle before I saw one of those white killing machines. Of course, nobody had mentioned black bears or grizzlies. Shivering at that thought, I knew I never would have made it in the Klondike and Yukon Gold Rushes. I knew I'd probably faint if I was ever confronted by one of those beasts and just curl up into a ball; meekly accepting that death was probable, if not inevitable.

I picked up the Jeep I had reserved and headed way over the Bow River en route to the motel; no hotel or inn on Vicenza's travel budget. "Besides," Vicenza had said, "this will get you to meet the real people in the north country." It had done that and while I had no real complaints on that score and was supremely grateful to have escaped the stifling urban atmosphere of New York, this "gig" just didn't look like it was for me.

While I did not miss the Big Apple, I did miss one of its millions of inhabitants: Ruth. I had recently developed the feeling that she would not have objected if I enhanced my "manliness" a bit. At least that's what I thought or, more accurately, what I told myself. I was what you could describe as a twenty-eight year old nerd.

I was no hero and really never wanted to be one. Sure, I had read my share of men's adventure series books like *The Executioner*, *Ashes*, and even the novels of Bond, James Bond. While I enjoyed Mack Bolan's one man war against the Mafia and God's warrior, Ben Raines as he battled communists, Nazis, and homegrown trash following a nuclear blasted America, this was the stuff of fantasy. There just couldn't be such heroic types in real life; right?

After two weeks of "communing with nature" and learning a lot of things I did not previously know or really didn't care to learn, I made my way through the customs lines one often runs into at airports, even in Calgary. While being able to visit various cities in Canada and Alaska as well as several of the mountainous states in the northern Rockies, and seeing the beauty of the Grand Tetons, the purpose of the trip had not been lost to me. I was returning to my old job. This kind of excitement and physical stress was not for Momma Rubenstein's little boy; no, not me!

I turned in all of "my gear" as it was called and settled in for the ride home; back to a saner and more civilized way of life.

CHAPTER TWO

Flying on a plane in those days always put me to sleep; I dozed off only to awaken with a start. Someone, a woman sitting in front of me, was screaming and a man I had noticed earlier was hollering at everybody else. I remember noticing this guy as we boarded, but we didn't speak. He had a certain "presence" that I sensed rather than felt. Our paths should have just "brushed up against each other's," never to have more significance, but that was not the way our lives were destined to be however. This was the first time I saw John Rourke in action.

The woman screamed again and grasped her throat with both hands. Rourke jumped up from his seat after ripping open his seat belt and shoved past a man in the seat beside him. Other passengers started screaming now. Rourke shouted, "Quiet down! This woman is having a heart attack, what's your excuse?"

The old woman was starting to gag. Rourke got her tongue back up out of her throat. A stewardess was at his elbow. "Are you a doctor?" she said.

"I trained as one. See if there's another doctor aboard. Hurry!" Rourke started bending toward the old woman, but stopped. He began hitting her chest. I heard the stewardess say, "What are you doing?"

Without looking at her, Rourke rasped, "I'm trying to get her heart started again." He kept at it for several seconds with no luck. "Stewardess!" he shouted.

"Yes, sir. There's no other doctor aboard. Can I help?"

Rourke glanced back, "Yeah. Find me a hair dryer and something to plug it into—hurry."

"A hair dryer?"

"Yeah," he rasped. "A hair dryer, electric razor—something like that."

She came back with a dryer; he grabbed it and ripped out the cord. Using a small pocketknife, he split the cord and stripped the insulation, exposing an inch of wire. "Plug this in when I tell you to—but don't touch these ends or let them drag against anything."

He ripped the old woman's dress down the front with both hands. "Okay— plug it in," he said. Taking the electrical cord, he made the ends spark. "Now," he whispered to the stewardess, "don't let anybody touch her." He touched both ends to the woman's chest; she bounced half off the seat. Leaning forward, he listened for her heart; he hit her again. Her body lurched up then back down into the seat.

"She's breathing!" the stewardess cried.

It was an amazing thing to watch. Ripping the electrical cord from the socket, he said, "Try to make her comfortable." Leaning down and listening to the woman's heart, he then held her wrist feeling for her pulse. "Keep her mouth clear. Have one of the passengers watch her to make sure her chest is rising and falling. And go tell the captain to set us down as soon as he can. This lady needs a hospital."

"I can give her oxygen."

"Save that for when she needs it—she's breathing okay for the moment," Rourke said. He pushed his way through the passengers and walked toward the center cabin bathroom, letting himself inside. He stayed there but a moment before retaking his seat. When the turbulence hit, John shouted, "Everyone look away from the windows and put your heads down! Protect your faces, your eyes!"

I don't think I had ever been more terrified. I looked down as he instructed. Later, John told me that as he was returning to his seat, he glanced out one of the windows and saw something in the air; something pale white and crashing down-ward. It was a missile, armed with a nuclear warhead; the city of St. Louis, Mis-souri vanished in the fire ball. I wondered how many lives had been snuffed out. What were their last thoughts? Did they feel the horror of knowing what was about to happen? Did they have time to say goodbye to loved ones, or was there simply a flash of blinding light followed by incineration and instant obliteration? I couldn't stop wondering.

After a few minutes, the turbulence eased; moans and cries were coming from passengers in the window seats who had their hands pressed to their faces. The stewardess who had helped him earlier came down the aisle, steadying herself against the jet's motion. Her face was white, her eyes wide; I overheard them talking. Rourke reached out and took her hand, leaning across the man next to him as he did. "What is it? You just came from the captain."

"Nothing, Mr. Rourke. Nothing to worry…"

Rourke stood up, stepping into the aisle, pulling a wallet from his hip pocket. He fished out one of his identity cards and handed it to her. "You know what this is?"

"It says Central Intelligence…"

"Yeah," Rourke whispered. "Now, unless your passenger list shows somebody else, I'm the closest thing to a government official you've got on this plane. Now, what's up? Pilot and co-pilot were blinded, weren't they?"

"How did you know?"

"Only makes sense. They couldn't have looked away from the St. Louis blast in time, too much glass up there anyway. Did the cabin keep its integrity; none of the glass was broken or anything?"

"Yes, but you're right. Neither of them can see. It's on autopilot now, but with this turbulence…"

"Exactly," Rourke said. "Give me the microphone for the speaker system," he said. He followed her up the aisle toward the front of the cabin and took the microphone. He said, "Ladies and gentlemen, my name is Rourke. I am a special employee of the government." Mutterings and exclamations mixed with the cries and sobs, and everyone began shouting out questions at once.

"Now," he said. "I want everybody to be quiet a minute and listen. First, pull down the curtains on the windows and don't look outside. Second, if you've got someone seated near you who appears to be having trouble with their eyesight, it should be just temporary," he lied. "After I'm through talking, get a pillow from the compartment above your seat and try to make the person comfortable. I'm also a qualified physician, so I will be coming around to check on you all. Take a blanket from the compartment and try to keep the injured warm. Soon, we will come to you and make available whatever medical assistance is required."

"It looks like the United States is under a nuclear attack," he added. There was another burst of cries. Someone started to scream. Rourke shouted over the microphone. "Now, let's be quiet and let's keep calm! I wish I could say something encouraging about what's going on below us on the ground, but I can't. But for now, we are all reasonably safe," he lied again.

"Now—I'd like anyone with flight training of any sort to report to the front of the forward cabin as soon as I'm through talking. Don't panic. The captain has the plane under control, but because of the turbulence from the heat on the ground, he can use some extra help on some of the instruments. Also, anyone with any sort of first-aid training or nursing experience, report up here as well, as soon as I'm through."

"We'll need your help to get everyone comfortable and start tending to their medical needs. The stewardesses will come around now with complimentary drinks. I suggest you have one. It's going to be a long night." Rourke handed the microphone to the stewardess.

Normally I was a teetotaler but when she came around with drinks, I ordered something I had only heard of—a Bacardi and Coke. I would end up having several more of them before the crisis was over. Several passengers started moving toward the front of the first-class cabin. Rourke addressed them all by saying, "Okay, let's crowd into the galley. Talk things over. You too," he said to the stewardess. When they had gathered, he told the stewardess, "Close the curtains and keep 'em closed," then turned to the rest. "Now, does anyone here have any kind of flight training?" A woman of about thirty raised her hand. The thin curtain blocked my vision, but allowed me to effectively eavesdrop.

"What kind of training?" Rourke asked.

I heard her respond, "I started private pilot training three weeks ago—I've had four lessons in the air. That's all."

"Well," Rourke said, smiling, "that's better than nothing, isn't it? Anybody else?" There was no response. Rourke said, slowly, "Then, I assume the rest of you have had some medical training. Now, the stewardess here will coordinate with you on what is needed and what we can get hold of to help. Anybody a nurse?"

Again, there was no response. "All right," Rourke said, "the stewardess is going to get on the PA system and see who among the passengers has aspirin or any other kind of painkillers. Lay off the aspirin unless nothing else is available. We might find that some of these people have radiation sickness and the last thing they need is something else to irritate their stomachs. Flush the burned areas on their faces and eyes; use cold compresses and try to make everyone comfortable. Do what you can. I'm a doctor, so if you need any advice, have the stewardess check

7

with me. Now, I don't have a bag or any instruments or drugs or anything, but I can help." To the woman who'd had taken flying lessons, Rourke said, "What's your name, Miss?"

"It's Mrs. Mandy Richards."

"Well, Mrs. Richards, you and I are going to go forward and see about helping the captain and the co-pilot. Okay?"

"I don't know how much help I can be, Mr. Rourke."

"Call me John. We'll help however we can." The stewardess was already starting back down the aisle with large containers of water and towels. The five who'd claimed some medical experience followed her. Rourke turned the handle to the pilot's cabin and then walked through. I could see past him inside the doorway; both the captain and co-pilot were still strapped into their seats. They held their faces and I think it was the co-pilot who was moaning.

"Shut the door, Mrs. Richards," Rourke said softly. She left the cockpit about thirty minutes later. I didn't see John Rourke again until after the plane crashed. I found out he had tried to land the plane, resulting in the crash. He had decided to try to land south of Albuquerque, reasoning there was a lot of flatland south of there, and the desert offered us the best chance of survival, figuring the Albuquerque airport was gone.

He told me later he had aimed for a flat stretch about five miles long with few trees and circled the area to burn off fuel and reduce the risk of fire. He ordered the stewardesses to get everybody off the plane as soon as we got on the ground. From my window, the plane was close to the ground now; it raced by as if the air speed were a hundred times faster than I had ever seen. I heard and felt the landing gear drop, but the right engines almost stalled. Then, they almost stalled again. John said over the public address system, "This is Rourke; brace yourselves for impact!" The plane slammed heavily into the ground. Rourke rasped, "We're down but not stopped. Stay in the crash position!"

It didn't seem the plane was slowing down at all; suddenly, it started to turn. "We're gonna hit!" Rourke shouted. The brakes seemed to hold for an instant then suddenly the plane lurched. I could hear the nose and the wings cutting into the trees. It sounded like a thousand chainsaws as they crashed down on the plane. It lurched again; trees were all around us and branches covered the front of the fuselage. Metal was being ripped apart; the noise was incredible and everything and everyone not tied down was bouncing around the cabin.

Suddenly, it was deadly still and quiet. "This is Rourke again. Get the hell out of the plane, but don't panic. Everything seems fine."

But, people were screaming—some were trapped in the wreckage. I saw John start back to help them when something on the floor caught his eye. I followed his gaze; he looked at it for a moment then turned away and leaned against the bulkhead. It was the severed head of the woman who had been in the cockpit with him, Mrs. Richards.

You know, all of these years later, I can still see Mrs. Richards' head; sometimes in my dreams, sometimes it just flashes in front of my eyes. No, the image is not my dreams—my nightmares.

CHAPTER THREE

I don't remember getting out of the plane or what happened after the crash. I think I just huddled with some of the other passengers, trying to stay warm in the cool desert air, and joined the others in a collective, shock-induced unconsciousness. My first real memories started the next morning when I saw John Rourke leaning against a rock, staring at the wrecked airplane. I walked toward him; his eyes were closed. He looked like he wanted to shut out the moaning of the injured passengers—the ones he'd worked on through the long day and night to save. A stewardess, the same one who had helped him on the plane, handed him a coffee cup. He thanked her and she said, "I don't believe the way you were able to get everybody out, Mr. Rourke, and then you went back for the things in the cargo hold. You're a real, live hero."

Rourke smiled at her. "Well, going back into the cargo hold was pure selfishness. I needed the stuff I had there." He had a pair of twin stainless pistols in the holster across his shoulders. "I'm going to have to go into town for some medical help—if I can find it. There isn't much more I can do for most of the people who are injured. When I leave you people, you may need to defend yourselves; and, I need to defend myself when I try making it into Albuquerque."

"Defend ourselves? From what? Surely, no one..."

My interest was piqued as I moved closer in to hear what he was saying to her. "Let me ask you a question," he said. "Would you have felt comfortable walking around in a high-crime area in Atlanta last night? Or any night?"

"Well, no."

"Well now, that's with police, civil courts, and the whole shot of civilization. What about with no police, no courts, no laws... no civilization?"

"But..."

"People who'd hit you over the head to steal your money when there might be a cop looking would definitely kill you to steal your food, your medical supplies, your ammunition—when their lives depend on getting it. You understand? Since last night, in almost any area you can think of, there is no law and no protection. The only recourse you have is yourself or someone who cares enough about you to put themselves on the line."

"Is that why you're going for help, Mr. Rourke?" the stewardess asked.

"Somebody has to," Rourke grunted. "I'm going to leave you in charge—with a gun. That Canadian businessman who was sitting next to me, what's his name?"

"Mr. Quentin?"

"Yeah well, he said that he shoots. I'll leave him a gun, also—two of them. If somebody shows up and starts acting funny, shoot first and ask questions afterward."

I remember thinking, *Well that's a tad harsh.* Yet, at the same time and for the first time in my life, I understood that kind of logic. I think that was what bothered me the most. At that exact moment, I understood. That didn't set well with me; I wasn't a barbarian. I had an above average memory. Details did not usually escape me but I didn't settle problems with force; I had learned the art of negotiation. I slid through life avoiding issues that were uncomfortable, untenable, and unsolvable. Was I changing?

Rourke continued telling the stewardess that he was taking some people with him and, that if they couldn't get any help to come out to the passengers, they would at least be able to bring back supplies. He told her that he would be back by late the next evening given that it was a twenty-five-mile hike to Albuquerque and then twenty-five miles back to the plane. "So just hold out, huh?" I heard him tell her.

Rourke showed her how to work the pistol and then left it with her. He gave his rifle to his florid-faced ex-seatmate, along with the snub-nosed revolver, reminding him the stewardess was in charge.

I guess you could say I was about to officially meet John Rourke; his analysis of our situation did not thrill me in the slightest. It seemed like, according to him, we had gone from incredibly bad to significantly worse. One thing I had already determined was unless he had some significant help, Momma Rubenstein's son, me, was looking like he could not survive. Hell, I thought it had been enough to survive a crash landing and the first attack of a nuclear war.

Rourke picked five of us; all men, he thought we would be strong enough and willing to accompany him on foot to Albuquerque. He asked us our last names and gave his estimate on the distance to travel and the amount of time it would take, but said that was only an estimate. I had already determined this guy knew what he was doing and he had far more experience in this type of activity than I did. Little did I know that before the end of this sojourn, I would be looking down the barrel of John Rourke's gun.

CHAPTER FOUR

He let one of us carry his rifle. The desert was cool with night falling. He pulled a sweater on over his shirt and pistols then put his sport coat back on. As we started from the camp, the stewardess ran after us. "Mr. Rourke! I thought you and the other men could use these." She handed him a paper bag.

"Sandwiches?"

"Uh-huh."

"Thoughtful, Miss . . ." Rourke had still not bothered to learn the young woman's name.

"Sandy Benson," she said, smiling.

"You have a pretty smile, Sandy," Rourke said, then turned and started away.

Hell, I thought, *maybe this guy does have a sensitive side.*

John glanced at his watch then at the hazy moon. Shifting a water bottle that hung over his shoulder with a borrowed trouser belt, he looked at us and then walked ahead of us. He told us that with rest stops, we'd be in Albuquerque by sunrise or before. We walked in silence for about an hour; each of us, I assume, lost in our own thoughts and fears before John called a rest stop.

We sat by ourselves and no one made a move to engage him in conversation; that seemed to suit John Rourke. I was more than ready for this break. Crossing a desert at night wasn't anything like trying to get across Seventh Avenue in New York's theater district—now that was exciting! Here in the desert, the cold and the stillness permeated not only your body, but your soul as well. Instead of the bright lights of the marquees beckoning you to come closer, you had only the glow from the silent stars above. Add to that my back and feet were hurting. Little did I realize that my "hurting" was nothing compared to the pain that was coming.

He watched us. There was O'Toole and Phillips; I don't think I ever knew the names of the others. One of the men, one of the two whose names I didn't know, suddenly said, "Are you really coming back, Rourke?"

"That's what I told everybody," Rourke answered quietly.

"Are you for real?"

"Why shouldn't I?" Rourke asked.

"Well, most of those people back there are dying, except for maybe the stewardess you left your rifle with, the Canadian guy, and a few others."

"Left my rifle, a CAR-15, with the Canadian; left the stewardess a Colt Python .357 revolver," Rourke corrected. "Don't you think we owe it to the people back there to help?"

"What about us?"

"Well, what about us?" Rourke asked him.

The one who had been talking started to get to his feet. "Well," he said, walking toward Rourke, "I say we don't."

Rourke stood; his back arching. "Then, just don't go back," he said. "We can get along okay without you."

"Yeah," the man said, stopping less than a yard from Rourke, "But that isn't the point. With your guns, we'd stand a better chance."

"I can see where that's true," Rourke said, looking away from the man a moment and nodding his head, "And you figure you need all the help you can get. Like my guns. Right?"

"Right."

The tension was palatable; it seemed like time was standing still. My nerves were definitely on edge. I didn't know what to expect, but I certainly did not expect what happened next. "Not right," Rourke said softly, and his left fist hammered forward into the man's stomach bending him at the waist. At the same time, his right knee came up, connecting with the side of the man's jaw.

So much for sensitive, I thought. Already, both of Rourke's hands had snatched one of the guns from the shoulder holsters. Rourke took a step back as one of the others had the stock of Rourke's rifle to his shoulder. Rourke shouted, "You might get off one shot but, while you're working that bolt action, I'll kill all of you unless that first shot is a good one. Your move; I've said my piece."

14

I stepped away from the other three, holding my hands in the air and saying, "Hey—wait. I'm not with them." The red-headed man with me, O'Toole, raised his hands saying, "Me neither!" John kept his guns trained on us and shouted to the others, "What about it?" The guy he had cold-cocked was starting to groan, and the one holding the rifle started to lower it.

"Don't drop it—set it down slowly," Rourke whispered. "Rubenstein." He had gotten my name right. I took a step toward him as he said, "Pick up my rifle. Grab it by the barrel, come here, and stretch it out to me. Be quick about it."

I followed the order exactly, picked up the rifle by the muzzle end, and started toward him, slowly. I had no doubt that, if he felt threatened, John Rourke would put a bullet in me and ask questions later. He shoved the pistol into his belt, reached out with his free hand, and grasped the stock of the rifle. He allowed the gun to slide through his hand until he could hold it just behind the trigger guard. Then he slipped it over his left arm by the sling, hanging the weapon on his left shoulder.

My hands and knees were shaking; I was scared to death. The man he'd knocked down was groaning louder now. John stepped back from him, looked at the four of us and spoke, "Now, if I were smart, I'd kill all of you right now and save myself headaches later on. Once we get into Albuquerque, anybody who wants to come into this with me and go back for the rest of the passengers can. Anybody who doesn't, just stay away from me. But if you split and if I ever see you again, I'll kill you. Now, you two." He gestured toward me and O'Toole, "Pick up this guy and get him walking. We're moving out and all you guys are staying in front of me. One wrong move from anybody and he gets a bullet; maybe two just for luck. Questions?"

There were no questions. O'Toole and I walked forward slowly and started helping the guy off the ground. John waved us forward with the barrel of his pistol and said, "All right, let's start walkin'." We did, and it didn't take long for the "adventure" part of this trek to wear off. I was used to thinking about miles in terms of minutes it required to travel them. There is a substantial difference between traveling by car and walking through what I would classify as the desert.

About halfway, I noticed a sensation coming from the heels of both feet. I realized that was probably the start of blisters and silently cursed myself for not wearing my hiking boots. At least they were broken in. But I had been headed

15

back to New York; I was ready to see Ruth and I wanted to look my best. All of that seemed somewhat trite now. Priorities had changed. Hell, the world had changed; I had no idea of what it was changing into, but I was about to change with it.

CHAPTER FIVE

It was almost four A.M. when we made it to Albuquerque; John said the sun would not be up for more than three hours. Except for lights from a church, Albuquerque's old town was gutted and burned. Whole streets had ripped apart when the firestorm hit natural gas lines. There was no electricity.

This was my first view of the war's aftermath. In a word, it was stark. It was devastation like I had never seen, even in the movies; but, more than the visuals, the smells and the silence haunted me. The silence was total; not a sound except the occasional wind and the crunch of our feet as we walked. The breeze brought whiffs of foul disgusting smells. I recognized spilled petroleum, burned wood, burned plastic, and burned metal. Others I could not distinguish—oh, and the smell of burning meat, luckily, all in the distance. *Thank God we made it!* I thought. My feet were killing me and I had developed a slight limp.

Stopping for several rests, the hike had taken us all night. I now sat on the ground and rested, as did the others. John looked like he could have made the return walk at any time. I saw no people, but I could hear the howling of dogs. "Well, I guess here's where we part company," John said, "at least those who want to. Looks from here like that Catholic Church is probably being used as a shelter. Anybody who's not coming with me back to the plane can split here."

He said he was going to check that shelter after taking care of a couple of things; he was going to find the closest thing to a hospital. He lit a cigar and said, "Anybody coming with me, step over here." For some reason I'll never understand, I was the first to move. I guess it was a toss-up between, "This is my only chance to survive" and "I wonder what it is going to be like?"

I'm sure Rourke was thinking, *Great, a smallish man with a receding hairline and wire-framed glasses.* John looked at me through a fog of cigar smoke as he exhaled. "What about you, O'Toole?" he asked.

"No. I don't want to go back," O'Toole said. "I don't know if I'm hanging in with these guys either, but I'm not going back to the plane."

"Suit yourself." Rourke wished O'Toole good luck. Turning to me, John said, "Well friend, let's go." We started across the fire-scorched square, picking our way over the large gouges in the pavement.

"Where are we going, Mr. Rourke?" I asked.

"It's John. What's your first name?"

"Paul."

CHAPTER SIX

"Well, Paul, Albuquerque is a town where a lot of people were interested in prospecting. Geology, things like that. So, I'm looking to find a geological equipment shop where there might be a Geiger counter. I want to see how much radiation we've taken. And then, we go back to the plane. I want to check out the rest of us."

I walked silently for a while and then asked, "Tell me, John, what're you going to do then, after we help those people back there?"

Rourke turned and looked at me, "Well, going back across the country to find my wife, Sarah, and our two children. They're back in Georgia."

I thought about that and said, "All those missiles that were going off around the Mississippi River, that whole area between here and Georgia are going to have created a huge desert, a big crater."

"I've thought of that," Rourke said slowly. "Here, turn down here." He moved onto the ruins of a side street. "There were a lot of little stores down here, I remember."

"I've never been to Albuquerque before," I admitted.

"It was a nice town," Rourke said, his voice low. "But anyway, I'll get back to Georgia—maybe work my way down through Mexico then up along the Gulf Coast. I'll have to play it by ear."

"What if they're dead when you get there?"

Rourke stopped in mid-stride and turned to me. "You married?"

"No, engaged, I have a girlfriend in New York and I have a mother and father in St. Petersburg, Florida."

"Are you going back for them?" He asked.

"I hadn't thought about it. I don't know."

He nodded and asked, "You got anyplace else to go, anything else to do?"

"No, I guess not."

"Neither have I," Rourke said. "I'm going on the idea that my wife and children are still alive. I'm going to look for them. And if they're not home—we had a farm in a rural part of the state—and if I don't find hard evidence that they're dead, I'll keep on looking."

"But aren't we all gonna die?" My voice was starting to crack.

"All of humanity wiped out? I'm not plannin' on it." At that, John turned and continued walking; he stopped a few yards further down what was left of the street in front of a partially burned building. "Well, look at that," he said, pointing up at the sign above it.

It read, "Geological Supplies." He pushed against the door; all the glass was broken out and the door moved in about a foot. He pulled a pistol from under his left arm and stepped through the doorframe; I followed close behind him.

Taking a quick glance around, I moaned, "This place is in ruins."

"Looks like but let's see," John said. The floor of the store was covered with charred pieces of wood, broken glass, and some half-burned small cardboard boxes. It looked like the fire had burned through quickly. The back portion of the shop was relatively untouched except for dark scorch marks on the walls.

"Jees," I said under my breath.

"What's the matter?"

"I tripped; this place is as dark as a closet."

"Just have to get your eyes accustomed," Rourke said quietly. "Close your eyes, count to ten, and then open them. There's moonlight from outside, enough to see by if you look close." It worked. "It looks like some sort of storeroom, back there, Rubenstein," John said.

"Where? That door?"

"Yeah. Watch your step now," he said as he picked his way across the rubble on the floor.

"It smells funny in here," I said.

"Well, it isn't gas. More like burned flesh," Rourke said, matter-of-factly.

"Burned what?"

20

"People, Rubenstein, people... Come on." He tried the doorknob, but the door didn't budge. Taking a step back, he raised his right leg and kicked. His foot smashed hard against the lock and the door fell inward.

"Just like in the movies," I remarked.

Rourke turned and looked at me, saying nothing. The storage room, high-ceilinged and narrow, was darker than the store had been. He waited in the doorway, letting his eyes become accustomed to the dimness.

"You must see real well in the dark," I said.

"I do, but it has its disadvantages. If I don't wear sunglasses when I'm outside during the day, the brightness gives me headaches—bothers my eyes." He started into the storeroom. "Here, just a second," he said, and in a moment, there was a soft clicking sound then a light. "Flashlight—they must have sold them here. I have to find batteries for them. Here," John said, handing the flashlight to me, "take this; I'll fix another one for myself."

"Isn't this stealing? I mean, couldn't we get shot as looters?"

"Yeah, we could," Rourke said, tightening his grip on the flashlight and flick-ing it on. "Not a very good flashlight," Rourke commented, flashing the angle headlight around the room. He stopped the beam at the high shelves at the back of the room.

"Look! What do you want for free?" I said, trying to be funny and braver than I felt.

"Yeah, I suppose you're right," he said. "Give me a leg up so I can get to that top shelf."

"What's a leg up?" I asked; I had never heard the expression before.

"Ten fingers, here," John said. "Put your hands together like that." Rourke put his right foot in my palms and then pushed himself up on the shelves.

"For a lanky guy, you're sure heavy," I gasped. John stretched to reach the shelf, got a grip on a box, and then slid down to the floor.

"What is that?" I asked.

Rourke brought down a Geiger counter. He dropped to his knees, ripped open the box, produced a dark-bladed knife, and pried at the cowling on the machine.

"What kind of a knife is that?"

"An A. G. Russell Sting 1A black chrome, it's a boot knife," John said absent-ly. "Hand me some of those batteries from the shelf up there—the big ones."

I handed him a half-dozen batteries; he took what he needed and said, "Hold onto the rest of them. You might find a couple more flashlights and get them working. See if there's anything else we could use. A couple of good-sized hunting knives wouldn't be a bad idea, and see if you can find some compasses. Oh, the knives... look for thick blades rather than long ones."

"Gotcha," I said and left the storeroom, while John finished placing the batter-ies and then replacing the cowling on the Geiger counter. Still stumbling, even with the additional light of my flashlight, I quickly looked around for extra flash-lights and some sturdy knives. I started to pick up a candy bar that was on a rack next to the front counter, but after a second or two decided to put it back. I didn't know if it was safe to eat after the blast, thinking it may be contaminated. I glanced back at it longingly then proceeded to complete my original mission.

When I returned, he was standing there naked wearing nothing but his guns and a knife. He had a strong, lean physique that was marred by scars, some puckered and round, some jagged; all looked like they had caused him great pain.

"You're naked!"

"Yeah, aren't I," he said. "I took a Geiger counter reading. My clothes and everything must have gotten contaminated up in the cockpit. But my sweater and my guns—everything from the cargo hold—were fine. I even had to ditch my watch."

"That was a Rolex wasn't it? That's about 1,500 bucks!"

"A radioactive watch won't do me much good. Besides, I've got another one back at the plane," Rourke said. "Here," he said, "I'm gonna sweep your clothes with the counter. You might be hot, too." He checked me with the wand of the Geiger counter and stepped back. "You should strip. Your clothes are contami-nated."

"But I can't run around naked."

"Your choice, friend," he said. "Would you rather get radiation poisoning?"

I started to undress and when I was naked, he ran the Geiger counter over me. "Get rid of your watch," he said.

"Sure," I said, "you threw away a Rolex; I can throw away a Timex. What the hell, huh?"

"Come on," he said. Rourke thought the next city block looked nearly untouched by the fire and that we might find a clothing store or something. I was right behind him as he started out of the store; damn, it was cold.

CHAPTER SEVEN

Either taking pity on this already turning blue semi-hairless specimen of a man or just wanting to get the show on the road, he tossed me his sweater. "And, watch your feet," he said. With the double shoulder holster across his back, the rifle slung from his shoulder, the Geiger counter in his left hand and the flashlight in his right, John started down the street seemingly unaware of his nakedness. His main concern, as he walked faster, was the howling sound some distance behind us.

"What's that noise?" I asked.

"Wild dogs—running in a pack," he said, his voice even.

"A pack of hungry wild dogs, huh?" I nodded. "And here we are, meat on the hoof, huh?"

"You've got the idea, Rubenstein," John said, smiling. "And, speak of the devil."

John stopped and turned; I was beside him now. At the end of the street less than fifty yards from us stood six dogs—five German Shepherds and one Doberman.

"My God," I whispered.

"The Lord helps those who help themselves, doesn't he?" John said, snatching one of the pistols into his right hand. He handed me the Geiger counter, the flashlight, and a bag of spare ammo he had taken from the store. "Here, hold my stuff," he said as he pulled the other pistol.

"You just gonna stand here?"

"Yeah," he said, "until they come at us in a run. Then, I'm going to shoot them. Here—take the rifle in case I miss one of 'em. Safety is off, all you have to do is pull it tight into your shoulder and squeeze the trigger."

"Oh," I said, "I never shot a gun in my life."

"First time for everything. Bet you never walked down the street naked before either."

"Well, yeah... you're right. First time for everything," I said.

He smiled as the dogs started edging forward. "How good a shot are you?" I asked, nervously.

"Not bad," he said. "Better than average, I guess," he added.

"Oh. You're not bad. Better than average," I laughed. "Well, listen. I'm glad of that," thinking that my life was hanging in the balance of what he had just said. I had this picture in my mind of the dogs running at me, knocking me to the ground, and each pulling on one of my extremities as if I were a giant chew toy. The dog I feared the most was eying my smallest extremity; a glint in his eye and drool running down his muzzle.

The dogs started into a loping run now, speed increasing as they closed on us. "Must be pretty hungry to attack people who look like they can defend themselves," John said slowly, raising the pistol in his right hand with the one in his left hand still hanging at his side.

"Must be," I said and took a step back. The nearest of the dogs—the largest German Shepherd—was thirty feet away when John fired. The round caught the animal square in the chest and it dropped. John raised the second pistol and he squeezed the trigger; the slug slammed into another dog that yelped once, ran a few paces, and fell. With the pistol in his right hand, he fired at the Doberman and missed. With the pistol in his left hand, he dropped the Doberman; the others were less than fifteen feet away now. John alternated firing; the gun in his right hand then his left. He fired both pistols at the last dog, dropping it in mid-air as it sprang toward him.

"That was spectacular!" I had never seen anything like that in my life; it was like a movie or something. He would have made one hell of a great cowboy in the Old West.

Rourke stooped over the nearest dog, studied it then stood, fished in the bag for spare magazines for his pistols, and then reloaded. "That dog has rabies," he said. Watch out for cats, dogs, anything. We gotta get out of here, soon." Without another word, we started down the street in our original direction. I slung the rifle across my shoulders.

On the next block, John stopped, stared up and down the street, and pointed. "Over there. We'll see if there's anything left—might have already been looted." He walked toward the clothing store with me behind. There was no glass left in the windows. Down the street, there was a huge hole where apparently a gas main had ruptured. Beyond that, at the end of the block, all the buildings were burned.

I asked, "Why are some of the buildings left and some only partway burned do you suppose?"

"A firestorm is a funny thing—it feeds on itself, builds its own winds. There's no logic to it. That's why they're so dangerous. Probably," said John as he cautiously stepped through the smashed glass door with his bare feet, "when that plane hit the gasoline tanker truck at the airport, the city was pretty much evacuated. They were probably expecting a Soviet missile to be targeted on them. No one to put out the fire so it got into the gas system and gas mains blew—then a firestorm. It must have burned itself out fast though."

"Here," I said, "take your flashlight," handing Rourke the light I had been carrying so he could have a better look inside the building. I followed him through the door, looking over my shoulder first, just in case there were more dogs following us.

"Thanks," Rourke muttered, shining the beam along the length of the store. "This particular establishment catered to a working class clientele from the looks of the clothing displayed. I don't see designer-style garments on the racks, just more or less your basic sturdy clothing that your mom would probably pick out for you. Help yourself," Rourke said over his shoulder, starting toward a table loaded with Levis. After ten minutes, we were dressed again—jeans, shirts, boots, and a jacket. I grabbed myself the warmest, thickest socks I could find and a pair of Red Wing hiking boots. With the thick socks, I figured I could break in the boots without a problem. Rourke walked behind the counter and from a smashed display case snatched a handful of Timex watches. "Here," he shouted, tossing a couple of the watches to me, and then put two on his left wrist.

"Got any idea what time it is?" I asked.

"Doesn't really matter anymore. A watch is just a way of keeping track of elapsed time. When the sun rises, it'll be about seven. Grab yourself a wide-brimmed hat, Paul," he added. "That sun on the desert will be strong tomorrow."

He snatched a pair of dark-lensed aviator sunglasses, tried them on, and then found a dark gray Stetson in his size.

Little did I realize that those glasses would be one of John's constant companions through the ages. "Let's head for that church and then find the nearest hospital," John said as we left.

I didn't have a better plan; I didn't have a plan at all, but John seemed to. I figured my best chance at survival... no, my only chance at survival was to stick close to him—and I did.

CHAPTER EIGHT

"I never wore a cowboy hat before," I told John, "except when I was a kid."
John turned as he started opening the door into the church. "Is that a fact?
Come on."

He stepped inside; I went in behind him. Immediately, we both turned back
toward the door; I started coughing. "My God, the stench!"

"Yeah, ain't it though," John said, turning back to look down the church's long
main aisle and toward the altar. The smell of burnt flesh was strong; pews had
been converted into beds with burn victims lined one after the other, head to head
along them as were the floors. John picked his way past the people in the aisles;
some were sitting up with open, festering sores on their beet-red faces.

Many of them had their eyes bandaged. There were six or seven nuns moving
about the church and near the front we saw a priest. John walked toward the man,
tapping him on the shoulder. The priest was gently washing the face of a little girl.
The hair on the left side of her head was burned away. Her face was a mass of
blisters. "Father," Rourke said.

The priest was dark and apparently Chicano; he glanced up and then turned
toward John. He looked like he hadn't shaved for several days. "Father, my name
is Rourke. My friend here and I are from a commercial jetliner that crashed about
25 miles south of here. I need to find a hospital, some medical..." but he stopped.
The priest's eyes were almost smiling, but not quite. John whispered, "This is the
hospital?"

"Yes," he responded. He told us that all the hospitals were destroyed in the
firestorm, they were doing what they could, and there must be thousands out there
in the ruins—like this one. "There is no one to help your people on the plane."

"What about medical supplies?" John asked.

"Water—and that is running out. We make bandages from what we can."

"I see," John said slowly, standing up. Then, he leaned over the little girl. He said, "Are you a doctor, Father?"

"We have no doctor."

John looked back at me and I nodded; his face set in a grim mask. "You do now—at least for a few hours. I'm a doctor."

"God has heard me," the priest said, making the sign of the cross and smiling. John ducked his head and at that moment I realized that John was something more than simply heroic; he was sensitive and compassionate. That realization would grow as we roamed the world together.

"Well, I can't say about that." John started working then until sunrise, then noon, and long into the afternoon. I did what I could to help, mostly applying water-soaked rags to some of the victim's burns, holding their hands, listening to their moans and, then sadly, carrying the dead outside.

Was I really much help? I doubt it; maybe all I really did was offer some comfort. Once, I helped the priest move one of the dead, a woman, into the courtyard behind the church. I stopped, stunned; it is difficult to describe what I saw and impossible to describe what I felt. I don't know how long I just stood there looking; time seems to have stopped in my memory. The priest finally cleared his throat and I looked at him. I was suddenly aware of the weight of the dead woman we were carrying. I looked at the priest... he looked at me... then we laid the woman on the ground. As we went back into the church, he put his arm around my shoulder. "Thank you my son for your help." I couldn't speak. I just nodded.

I had never seen such suffering, such absolute agony... the elderly, the children... people my age. The dead, the dying... the living. The living were the worst I think, locked in suffering that no one should have to endure. There were horrific injuries, missing limbs, charred burned flesh, yet there were others who seemed to have no injuries at all. They sat in stoned silence, isolated from time and humanity with their minds seared beyond repair by the horrors they had witnessed.

The hours we spent there seemed both as minutes and as days; my senses weren't numbed... they simply ceased to function. There were dozens of bodies in the yard when Rourke walked over to the priest, "Father, I'm going to have to get back to the plane now."

Finally I thought, feeling both relief and shame for thinking it, *It is over.*

"Yes. I have been waiting all afternoon for you to say this. I knew you would have to return to the airplane. May God go with you," the priest told him. "You have helped—and God bless you for it."

John took the priest's outstretched hand then turned to go. He stopped and cast a questioning glance at me over his shoulder. "I'm coming, John," I said.

He turned to me, holding his hat in his hands, saying, "After all this time, I don't know what we'll find out there, Paul."

"I know that," I said. "I'm going with you anyway." I thought about what he said, '... I don't know what we'll find.' I thought, *It can't be any worse than this.* I was wrong.

CHAPTER NINE

John just nodded and turned. It was dark again by the time we reached the edge of the city and much colder. The howling of the wild dogs had grown louder with the falling darkness. Much of the residential section here had not been burned, but was deserted.

"Where do you suppose everyone went?" I asked.

"Up there," he answered, pointing toward the mountains on the other side of the city. "For some reason, whenever there's disaster, people always think of going to the mountains. Santa Fe is probably a giant refugee center by now. It doesn't look like there were any hits up there either."

"Why don't we go to Santa Fe for help then?" I asked.

"Too far to walk, and if the town is still functioning, I'd guess they don't have any doctors, nurses, or medical supplies to spare."

"Okay," I said, "I have to ask. How come you're a doctor but you run around with guns?"

He grunted, "That's a long story."

"I got the time."

So he told me how he had studied to be a doctor, went all through college and medical school, and even interned. But then he started watching what was happening in the world and realized that, as a doctor, all he'd be able to do would be to patch things up for other people. He thought that maybe in the CIA, or something like that, he could keep things from needing to be patched up for a while longer. After a few years in covert operations, down in Latin America mostly, he saw that wasn't possible.

Rourke had always been into guns—hunting, the outdoors, the whole nine yards, and started getting interested in survivalism. He was a weapons expert already and found himself writing articles and books on guns, knives, and all kinds of related accessories. He then started getting into the technical side of survival. He found out there was a lack of books on the subject and that many of the books available had misinformation; he thought it could be dangerous if the reader took it seriously.

Because of his degree, he wound up doing a lot of seminars on survival medicine, stuff like that. He traveled all around the United States, parts of Latin America, the Mideast, and Europe teaching survivalism and weapons training, while researching for his next book.

We walked on in silence. As we passed a house on our left, John stopped me. We were more or less in suburban Albuquerque by now, close to crossing over into the desert once again. John pointed at a house, well-kept with a nicely landscaped front yard. It seemed totally intact with a garage at the end of a long driveway; the door was closed all the way. "Look at that," Rourke said, "and see if you're thinking what I'm thinking."

He didn't wait for a reply but sprinted up the drive toward the garage. He tried the garage door; it was locked. He jerked one of the pistols from his shoulder holster. Yes, I now know they are called Detonics but I didn't know what to call them in the beginning. "I'm going to shoot the lock off—get out of the way," he said; he took aim and fired once. The lock and most of the handle fell away, but the door was still not accessible.

"Go find something to pry at this door with," he said, but I returned empty handed.

"What's the matter?" he asked.

I grinned, feeling so proud of myself. Yep, I was the man! "I found something better than a pry bar," I said, smirking. "The side door is unlocked."

"Did you look inside?"

"Yeah." I said. "The prettiest '57 Chevy you ever saw. It's up on blocks, but the tires are there."

John followed me into the garage. A tarpaulin was draped half over the gleaming fire-engine red and chrome vintage car. "Look for some gas," he said, in a near whisper. Ten minutes later, we had three two-gallon gas cans and were putting the wheels on the car. Working now on the last wheel, John said, "Here," then handed me one of his pistols. "Take this and look around the block. See if you can find any more gas. That's the gun I used on the door. It's only got five rounds left in it. If I hear you shoot, I'll come running."

I thought to myself, *I bet I'll be running faster.*

While I was gone hunting, John finished the wheels and started working on the garage door until he had released the locking mechanism. He checked the battery and the radiator, adding some water. He found the key under the front seat and tried the ignition. The car groaned a few times. He knew if the battery was dead it was hopeless. That's when I returned with one more can of gas.

"Good," he muttered. "If this battery doesn't turn this over, you can go out and check for a battery and tools to change it with. Keep your fingers crossed," he added. He looked at the key, turned it and whispered, "Come on baby—this'll be the ride of your life." The engine coughed and then roared as he stepped on the gas pedal.

"Yahoo!" I shouted.

John looked up at me with a squint in his eyes against the flashlight he held. "You're takin' that cowboy hat awful serious, aren't you? Come on, Paul, pour in that gas and let's get out of here." He looked over at me and smiled. "Let me guess. You've never stolen a car before—or ridden in a '57 Chevy? Right?"

"Yeah," I grinned. "How'd you know?"

"Intuition," he said as he laughed, hauling the big long-throw gearshift into first. "Intuition." The needle on the speedometer bounced near twenty as he slowed at the end of the long driveway. He let up on the clutch again and made a hard left into the street. He raced through the street, turning onto one of the major arteries.

"You just ran a ..." I started but then fell silent, smiling to myself.

"I don't know about you," John said, "but right now, I'd be happy if a cop pulled me over for a ticket." He glanced at me and I nodded.

I had just settled in for our ride across the desert when I noticed, "Hey—this thing's got a tape deck."

"Wonderful," John said. "Check the glove compartment and see if he's got any tapes."

"Found one," I said as I inserted a cartridge.

As the music began, we looked at each other. "The Beach Boys?" John asked.

"You gotta admit," I said, touching the dashboard, "the music goes with the car." We were driving instead of walking and we had music instead of silence. For a while it seemed like everything was back to normal, I can't describe how good it felt. Trouble was, I knew that feeling wasn't going to last very long.

CHAPTER TEN

John reminded me that by now I had played that tape all the way through—twice. I laughed, I think for the first time in front of him. I should have felt guilty for laughing but it felt good. I needed a release from all the tension that had been building inside. I pulled the tape from the deck and said, "I know this sounds horrible with all that's happened—I mean World War III began two days ago. But here I am, wearing a cowboy hat and riding in a fire-engine red '57 Chevy, out to rescue some people trapped in the desert. Two days ago, I was a junior editor with a trade magazine publisher and dying of boredom. Maybe I'm crazy—and I'm sure not happy about the War and all—but I'm almost having fun."

John nodded. "I can understand."

"Two days ago, I needed help. Today, I'm helping. I've done more in the last two days than I've done in the twenty-eight years I've been alive."

"You twenty-eight?"

"Yeah—last month. I look older, right? Everybody tells me that."

John laughed. "I wasn't going to tell you that. You look twenty-eight to me."

"Well," I started to say, but John held up his hand and ground the Chevy to a halt. "What is it?" I asked.

"Listen," Rourke said. "Gunfire. Just down the road and off to the right there. Sounds like it's from the plane." We had been speeding down a dirt road for the last ten miles. When he heard the gunfire he slowed down and punched the lights off. As we neared the crash site, he killed the engine; the sound of the gunfire grew louder. He eased the car to the side of the road.

"Paul, you want one of my pistols, or the rifle?" For no reason than it was one of only two choices, I chose the rifle. John reached into the backseat, removed the scope cover, and showed me where the safety lever was. I worked the bolt and introduced a round into the chamber. Fishing in his pockets, John found the two spare five-round magazines for the rifle and handed them to me.

"Just look through the scope, pull it tight into your shoulder. When you see the image clearly—with your glasses on—it should pretty much fill the scope. Get the crosshairs over your target and squeeze the front trigger. You'll be a terror with it. Come on."

John threw open the driver's door and started running toward the rocks; I followed right behind him. The sound of the gunfire was dying now and above it, we could hear muted voices calling back and forth to each other. By the time we had climbed up into the rocks and looked down onto the flatland below, the gunfire had totally ceased. I immediately knew we were too late.

John reached under his coat and stripped a pistol from under his left shoulder with his right hand. He had two more full magazines with him. "They're starting to move out," he said, peering toward the campsite. As best as he could tell, all the passengers had been killed.

The bikers, two dozen of them, were going through the baggage. We watched as they came to the body of a woman. We couldn't be sure but we thought it was the stewardess, Sandy Benson. One of the bikers bent over her and took John's own glinting pistol from the ground beside the woman.

"Give me the rifle," John whispered. Taking the rifle and spreading his feet along the ground, he pulled the butt into his shoulder and squinted through the telescopic sight. He settled the crosshairs and pulled the first of the twin, double-set triggers. I saw the man stand and whirl around. John squeezed the trigger. The rifle rocked against his shoulder; the biker's forehead split like a ripe melon. The man's body flipped backward in a heap on the ground. I was trying to follow the movement of the rifle. John was quietly identifying his targets, unconsciously I think.

As the other bikers started to react, he leveled the rifle again. A biker wearing a Nazi helmet threw his hands to his chest and fell back, his bike collapsing to the side as his body hurtled over. John worked the bolt again and said, "Woman biker, arms full of belongings of the dead passengers." I spotted her running across the camp as John swung the scope. A bald biker on a big, heavily-chromed street machine waved frantically for her.

As she reached out to touch the hand of the bald biker, Rourke fired, killing the bald man. The man's head exploded, resulting in bits of bone, hair and flesh flying in every direction as if they were fireworks on the Fourth of July. Quickly cocking the bolt, he swung the scope to the woman. I couldn't hear her above the sounds of the motorcycles revving in the camp area now, but it looked like she was screaming. She dropped to her knees and he shifted the scope downward a few degrees, pulling the trigger. I could see a crimson red hole in her forehead and a bloody spray blow out the back of her head. Her body snapped back.

John swapped magazines on the rifle, worked the bolt action, and shot another biker in the right side of his neck. His bike half-climbed a small rise then rolled over. John worked the bolt again and swung the scope onto another biker saying, "Nazi helmet." John fired. The rifle round splattered against the right side of the helmet—the biker threw his hands up and fell off. He rolled over and laid still.

John worked the bolt, spotting another biker. Almost under his breath he said, "Sleeveless denim jacket with a gang name across its back." The biker crawled along the ground before breaking into a dead run for a group of bikers to John's left. He fired and hit the biker in the back. The impact threw the man's body forward on his face and into the dirt.

He's calling his shots like in a pool game, I thought. Then John moved the scope, working the bolt action fast and ripped the last three shots into the group of bikers the last man had been running toward. Three bodies fell. Three others jumped onto their machines. John swapped magazines again and brought the rifle back to his shoulder, firing twice and killing two more as their machines moved out of the campsite. He brought the rifle down from his shoulder and clicked the safety on.

I couldn't believe what I had just witnessed. I inhaled and then slowly let it out, having forgotten to breathe while watching this poetry of death scene playing out in front of me. I was lying on the rocks beside him and said, "You just killed twelve men!"

"No," John said, "Eleven men and one woman." We proceeded down from our hiding place to see if any of the passengers were still alive. He tossed the rifle to me and started running along the rocks down toward the campsite. The wind caught his Stetson, blowing it from his head. He reached under his coat and snatched out one of the pistols, in case any of the bikers had survived, I assumed.

As he reached the flat space beneath the rocks, he broke into a crouching run toward Sandy Benson.

I stumbled along behind him as fast as I could. Halfway there, I realized I didn't have any pain in my feet. Blisters just seemed out of place with the death and devastation that lay before me. The death and devastation just got worse the closer we came to the plane and the bodies.

Not only could I see the blood and broken bodies but I could smell them. I never knew before you could smell blood, bowels, and bladders that empty when death arrives; you can however, and it is a smell that doesn't leave you. There is also a smell that comes hours and days after death: decomposition. It's an even a worse smell; it permeates your skin, your hair, and your clothes.

Once you have smelled it, it is branded on your senses. You never forget it, at least I never have.

CHAPTER ELEVEN

Rourke dropped to his knees beside the stewardess, rolled the body of the dead biker away, and leaned over her. He raised her head in his hands. She opened her eyes. Her blonde hair fell back from her face as she looked up and smiled at him.

"Like I told you before—you got a pretty smile, Sandy," John said.

"I knew you'd come—I knew it, Mr. Rourke." Her head fell back and after a moment, John bent over and kissed her forehead. Tears filled my eyes as I watched John tenderly close her eyelids with the tips of his fingers then rest her head back down on the ground. I moved away to see if there were any survivors nearby. He found his pistol, the Python, beside her in the dirt, picked it up and opened the cylinder. All six rounds had been fired. John searched through her purse, finding the two speed loaders he'd left with her; he emptied one into the gun, tossing the empty cases into his pocket. As I walked up behind him, he looked up. Standing, he blew the sand from the big Colt revolver, closed the cylinder, and stuffed the gun in his waistband.

"I found Quentin—the Canadian. He's dead. I checked some of the others. I think they're all dead," I said to him.

"Will you help me here?" John asked, looking down at the dead girl by his feet. "I want to haul all the bodies up by the plane then torch the plane. We can't possibly bury them."

"The bikers too?" I asked.

"I wouldn't spit on them," he said.

The makeshift funeral pyre took more than an hour for the two of us to construct. Before we set the plane ablaze, John went through the belongings of the passengers and the dead bikers for anything we could use. We placed everything we might use in a pile in the center of what had been the camp. He told me to wait for a few moments and then left. When he returned, he had his flight bag and gun cases. "I stashed these," he said, "back on the other side of the plane."

"You always plan ahead, don't you John?"

"Yeah, Paul," he whispered. "I try to."

I was still half in shock; I could not get over the mass slaughter committed by the bikers. More than forty people had been murdered for no reason. John changed into his own clothes from the flight bag, packing the clothes he'd taken in Albuquerque inside it. He wore a pair of well-worn blue denims, black combat boots, a faded light-blue shirt, and a wide leather belt. Having nothing besides my city clothes somewhere strewn in the immediate area, I chose to remain dressed in my newfound Albuquerque wardrobe. Comfort before style became my new motto.

CHAPTER TWELVE

John squinted toward the rising sun through his dark glasses. He had a camouflage-patterned gun belt with the Python nestled in it on his right hip. The double shoulder rig was across his back and shoulders like a vest; magazine pouches for the twin .45s on his trouser belt.

The Sting boot knife was inside the waistband of his trousers on the left side. He took the gun I had found on the Canadian, Quentin. Quentin had died with the little revolver locked in his right fist. John placed it inside his flight bag. Walking over to the bikes that were left, John selected a big Harley and strapped the flight bag to the back of it. Then, he slid his rifle into a padded case and secured it to the side of the bike. All the time, I kept nervously talking, "I'm goin' with you. You're goin' after the rest of the bikers, aren't you?"

"Yeah," Rourke said, pulling the leather jacket on against the predawn cold that still clung to the desert. Finally, John turned to me and said, "Can you ride one of these things or do you want the car?"

"Pick out a motorcycle for me and show me how to work it. Hey, I was thinking about what you said earlier. My parents, in St. Petersburg, maybe they're alive; maybe they could use my help. And, I wasn't much good back there against the bikers. Maybe I could learn to be better. I want to get them too." I had been thinking a lot about this and I meant every word that I said. I was through with just being an observer. I'd had a taste of what life could be if I was willing to learn how.

John looked down to the ground. He checked his spare Rolex in the winking sunlight on the horizon. "Let's call it 7:15," he said. He walked over to the pile of weapons and accessories by the burnt-out fire.

"One of 'ems got my CAR-15," he said absently as he picked up a World War II vintage submachine gun from the pile and handed it to me. Sifting through the debris, he came out with four thirty-round magazines. "Call this a Schmeisser; its real name is an MP 40," he said. I did and have called it that through the ages.

"Can I come with you?" I asked.

John smiled and just said, "Wouldn't have it any other way. Now, like I asked before," as he gestured toward the motorcycles, "you know how to ride one of these things?"

"Nope," I grunted, shaking my head.

John sighed hard. "Can you ride a bicycle?"

"Yeah."

"Good. I'll show you how the gears and the brakes work. You'll catch on. Between New Mexico and the East Coast lies more than 2,000 miles. You should get the hang of it. Now, give me a hand here." We scrounged some .38 Special ammo that he said would also work in his .357 revolvers and some additional .308 ammo in the process. "Should I take a handgun?"

"Yeah, you won't need a rifle. Once I get my CAR-15 back, we'll have two. Here, use this for now." He reached into the pile and found an automatic. "This is a Browning High Power, a 9mm. One of the best there is." I took the gun and John helped me find a holster that would work with it.

We siphoned off gas from the other bikes to fill the tanks of the Harleys John had chosen for us. Siphoning gas was something I was becoming an expert at. At this stage, anything I could add to my resume was a plus. I gathered my belongings and strapped them on the bike; Rourke took the remaining loose ammo from his gun cases—which he was leaving behind—and replenished the magazines for his pistols and the rifle, packing away the spare magazines for his CAR-15 for when he got it back.

Finally, we were ready. Foodstuffs from the airplane were our only provisions. Rourke checked it all with the Geiger counter. We were low on water, so we took the two-day-old coffee as well. Then, filling every container we could find with gasoline from the remaining bikes, we prepared the crashed aircraft for the funeral pyre.

Standing well back, John took a gasoline-soaked rag and started to light it, but I stopped him. "Aren't you gonna say anything over them?"

"You do it," John said quietly.

"I'm Jewish; most of them weren't."

"Well, pick something nondenominational," he said.

I coughed and then began, "The Lord is my shepherd. I shall not want. He maketh me to lie down in green pastures. He leadeth me beside the still waters. . ."

John, almost without realizing it, joined in, "He restoreth my soul."

I turned and looked at John, and we both went on. "He leadeth me in the paths of righteousness for His Name's sake. Yea, though I walk through the valley of the shadow of death, I will fear no evil, for Thou art with me." My thoughts were filled with images of Mrs. Richards and Sandy Benson, whose courage had seemed unending.

"Thou preparest a table before me in the presence of mine enemies; Thou anointest my head with oil. My cup runneth over. Surely, goodness and mercy shall follow me all the days of my life..."

John closed his eyes, and I knew his thoughts were of his wife and their children at that moment. Were they even alive? "And I shall dwell in the house of the Lord forever."

John opened his eyes and saw me turn to face him. "You've gotten all the rotten jobs, John. It's my turn now. Give me the torch." He said nothing; he handed me the gasoline-soaked rag then the lighter. "Be careful," he said then watched as I took his battered Zippo lighter, rolled the striker wheel and touched the flame to the rag. In an instant, the rag was a torch; I threw it into the gaping hole in the fuselage. At first, I was afraid the flame had gone out. The plane didn't look any different, just dark, hulking, and broken. I heard a tiny crackling sound like cellophane being rubbed between two fingers; then, it started to get louder, more like bubble wrap popping. A faint yellow-blue glow could be seen deep down inside the hole, growing ever so slightly as I continued to stare, mesmerized. The flames grew taller, their arms reaching out grasping, beckoning. The smoke turned from white to black and billowed from the broken windows and breaks in the fuselage.

"Come on," John rasped, his voice suddenly tight and hoarse. I was still standing by the plane and John walked up to me and put his hand on my shoulder. "Come on, Paul. We've got work to do." I looked at Rourke, took off my glasses for a moment, but said nothing. The sound of the flames from the plane was all there was for either of us to hear. The sound was bad enough; what I had not anticipated was the smell that hit us when the wind shifted a few minutes later.

Down the road we stopped to take a leak; something got my attention, but it was like a wisp on the wind. There was the scent of petroleum and the scent of cooking meat. I recognized it from the hospital in Albuquerque where all of those people were stretched out on church pews; blistered, burned, and dying.

It was worse than the smell I had experienced when we first got to the plane. It was nauseatingly sweet; I'm ashamed to admit it, but at first, it smelled good... then, I realized what it was. I threw up and in a few seconds, I threw up again. I literally felt like I was turning inside out. As bad as that was, when my stomach had nothing else to give up, the dry heaves started and they were worse.

CHAPTER THIRTEEN

The ride across the desert had been hot. I had managed to only fall off the big Harley once, but wasn't hurt; that is if you don't count "road rash," some banged knuckles, and a wrenched up knee. As we stopped on a low rise John turned to me, saying, "I think you're getting the hang of it, Paul. Good thing too. Look." He pointed down into the shallow, bowl-shaped basin before them.

"My God!" I said, shuddering. There in the basin that was once a lake bed but now just sand and barrel cactus, were the bikers we had been trailing. John recognized, even from a distance, two of them from the clothes they wore. One man in particular, whom he had picked as the leader of the gang, wore a Nazi helmet with steer horns jutting from each side; not unlike a Viking helmet. None of the other bikers in the basin had such a helmet. There were at least forty of them.

"What is it—some kind of convention?"

"What?" John asked absently. Then, realizing what I had said, he commented, "They were probably part of a larger biker gang and they all set this spot as a rendezvous point. Could be more of them coming."

"Damned bikers." I spat in the dust.

"Hey—we're bikers now, aren't we?" John said, looking at me and taking off his sunglasses to clean the dust from them. He went on, "Most bikers are okay—some of them are bad-asses but you can't generalize. Just 'cause somebody's got a machine under him and he doesn't much care for authority doesn't make him scum. It's just these guys—they are scum."

"But there's gotta be almost three dozen of them down there."

"I make it forty, give or take," John said lazily, checking his watch and then checking the sun. "In another two hours, it'll be dark. Looks like a good moon tonight though. We'll get 'em all then."

Working the numbers quickly in my head, I realized that we were talking twenty-to-one odds. "There's just two of us," I thought to mention to John.

"Yeah. At least they can't accuse us of taking unfair advantage of them."

"Twenty-to-one, John?"

"Remember what you said over the men and women they killed back at the plane? 'Yea, though I walk through the valley of the shadow of death, I will fear no evil.' Well, I never cared for fearing things—doesn't help anything much." Then, pointing to the desert behind them, he said slowly, "See all that Paul? Now that's something we're never going to cross in fear. What's out there in that country after the war, neither of us knows. Nuclear contamination, bands of brigands that'll make these suckers down in the basin look like sissies, probably Russian troops. I don't have the idea that we won the War, really. God knows what else."

There'll be plenty of chances to be afraid later, I figured. *No sense starting before we have to.*

As quietly as we could, we parked our Harleys behind the cover of some large rock outcroppings, ate some of the food we'd brought from the plane, and rested. John filled me in on his plan. When he finished, I said, "You're gonna get killed." He just shrugged.

We waited until past sunset and well into the night. The moon was up and the sounds from the biker camp in the basin indicated that everyone was pretty well drunk. While we waited, another half-dozen bikers had come into the camp.

I watched as John checked both of the stainless pistols, checking the spring pressure on the magazines, hand-chambering the first round rather than cycling it from the magazines of the guns. This gave him six rounds, plus one in each gun, plus the spare magazines. He secured the pistols in the double Alessi shoulder rig then slipped the massive two-inch Colt Lawman inside his trouser belt at the small of his back.

He told me it was Metalifed (I had no idea what that meant) like the Colt six-inch Python on his right hip. The gun belt had loaded dump pouches, but he was counting on speed if he had to reload. For that, he had something called Safariland cylinder-shaped speed-loaders; there were four of them. They were designed for use with the Python, but worked equally as well with the Lawman two-incher. He put two of each in the side pockets of his jacket. Taking a swig of the old coffee, he stood up and walked toward his bike.

"I still say you're crazy."

"Could be," he said, settling back and lighting a thin dark cigar with that old battered Zippo. "You know, I'm almost out of cigars. Hope we find some place that's got some one of these days." He sucked deeply on the cigar. "Don't forget to get down there with that Schmeisser when I need you." I stuck out my right hand; John looked at me, smiled, and shook it. Then, he cranked the bike and headed out from behind the rocks and down into the basin. He kept the bike slow as he rode it down.

Glancing from side to side, I could count perhaps fifty bikers, most of them lying about on the ground. I lay there out of sight, unsure of what was about to occur and not sure I was ready for any of it. Before today, the only gun I had ever fired was a brand new Fanner 50 cap gun my dad had given me for my twelfth birthday. While I was "deadly" with it, it was a toy and this was no game. As a child, I played Cowboys and Indians but being shorter than the other kids and darker—I was always the Indian. I was constantly getting the crap beat out of me by the other guys. One day, I discovered a hero I could play: Tonto—the Lone Ranger's Indian sidekick and I was set.

Today, however, my Lone Ranger was riding down into a hornet's nest and I was sitting there watching it. In all honesty, my mouth was dry and my hands were shaking and sweaty—a condition John told me later was absolutely normal. I don't remember having any clear thoughts at the moment; everything was swirling around in my head. I guess you could call it a form of sensory overload since I wasn't sure what to do... I was more or less on autopilot.

I could see the glint of broken wine and whiskey bottles reflecting in the moonlight around the campsite. There were guns everywhere. I couldn't tell what kind they were, but John would have known. Everyone I could see wore at least one handgun; several had two. As John reached the campsite and started in, I saw some of the bikers get to their feet and watch him.

John slowed the bike as he reached the center of the camp, but kept the engine running, stopping less than three yards from the big man with the horned Nazi helmet. He was sitting with his back to his machine. A woman was on each side of him. John took a deep drag on his cigar and said something I couldn't hear. The Viking stood up and hitched his jeans up by the wide black belt slung under his beer pot belly; they were talking now.

Someone shouted, "He's ridin' Pigman's bike!" With the cigar in the left corner of his mouth, I could see John squinting against the smoke. The Viking stepped closer toward John. John, I couldn't hear him but he told me later he whispered, "I just wanted to make sure you knew who I was." His left hand had been resting on the back of the bike seat when he flashed it outward; the snub-barreled Lawman appeared in his fist.

He pulled the trigger twice. The muzzle was less than a yard from the Viking's face and both bullets sliced through his head; blood and brains exploded, spattering the two women who began to wail and run. The battle was on and I was about to join in.

CHAPTER FOURTEEN

John gunned the Harley and started into the wall of bikers in front of him, firing the Lawman empty at the nearest of them. He rammed the empty revolver into his belt and started firing the Python. The bikers fell away from him like a wedge; the Python's slugs roaring into faces, chests, and backs. He was a killing machine on two wheels. They had been standing so tightly together that missing one was impossible. As he reached the far end of the camp, John jerked the bike into a tight circle, skidding as he went and dismounted. Already, there were bikes revving up from inside the camp. A swarm of the bikers started toward him, on foot. Crouching beside the bike, he speed-loaded the Lawman and Python, setting them comfortably in his hands.

I took a deep breath, checked the Schmeisser and then was up and on my way down to him, running for all I was worth. I saw a man in dirty denim with a bare chest pointing a pistol directly at my forehead; the barrel looked like it was the size of the opening on a galvanized trash can (at least that was the impression I had.) He was still fifty feet from me when I opened with the submachine gun. I pointed and pulled the trigger.

I moved the gun back and forth in an arc—like I had seen gangsters do in the movies. I unloaded a full magazine in his direction. Riding the recoil of the Schmeisser, I saw four slugs impact his chest; he fell back. Four rounds out of a thirty-two-round magazine; I had just killed my first human being. I rammed a fresh magazine in the Schmeisser and pulled the Browning out with my left hand.

I was running again and shouting above the gunfire below—the same counterfeit Rebel yell I'd made back in the garage when we'd gotten the '57 Chevy started. The terrain was treacherous and several times I feared my feet were going faster than I was. I was scared to death, but... I also never felt more alive.

John was firing his revolvers at the bikers, putting away the empty revolvers as he advanced toward the center of the camp. He snatched up an M-16 from the ground where it had been dropped by a dead biker. Walking toward the center of the camp, he fired the assault rifle empty then snatched up a Thompson submachine gun nearby him on the ground.

I hit the flat ground and was still running when I opened up with the Schmeisser. I had already killed my first man and was about to kill another. Strangely, I felt... I guess the word was... detached. It was like I was watching someone else doing what I was doing. I lost track of John at that point and, for a while, my focus was simply to kill or be killed. I wanted to avenge those poor souls we had incinerated in the plane's carcass.

I fired out the Schmeisser and dropped to my knees beside my bike to reload; glancing up I saw John again. Don't ask me what was happening. To be honest, I don't really remember much; I was doing something I had never had to do—fight for my life. As I fumbled loading the next magazine, I saw John snatch up a 12-gauge riot shotgun which one of the bikers had dropped; he worked the pump, chambering a round. He hauled up a motorcycle from the ground, straddled it, and started the engine. From behind him, I shouted, "Rourke—what are you doing?"

He pulled the motorcycle around, charging after the one survivor of the camp, and shouted back, "I'm not finished!" Passing the perimeter of the camp, he started picking up speed. The biker's dust trail faded ahead of him. The basin was far longer than it was wide and at the distant end toward where John headed was a steep hill. When he was within range; Rourke fired only one shot—the last biker was down.

I don't know how many men I killed in those few minutes. When the firing stopped, I reloaded the Browning and stuck it in my belt. As I made it back to where we had parked, I slipped a fresh magazine in the Schmeisser, hung it across my neck, got on my bike and looked for John. He was walking back toward the camp when he saw me. He stopped and switched loads in his .45's as I waited. I slowed the bike; I was still having a hard time controlling it. As I finally got it stopped, the machine nearly skidded out from under me. John waited a moment until the dust settled. Then, he walked over to me and the bike. I asked very softly, "Are you finished now?"

John nodded his head, saying, "We've got a long ride ahead of us, but I'm finished for now." We retrieved his Harley, mounted up and headed toward the east; I don't remember exactly when the shakes started, about thirty to forty-five minutes into the ride. At first, I thought the weather was cooling off and I was getting chilled, but that wasn't it at all.

When you're riding a motorcycle, any motorcycle and traveling any distance, you have a lot of time to think; there's not much else to do. I was thinking; boy was I thinking. I had just faced death and I had just killed someone, probably several. I had survived with no clear vision of how.

All of a sudden, it all came back to me in vivid details; colors were brighter and sounds were clearer—this had never happened to me before. I realized I had survived, not because of anything I had done, not because of any training I had and not because of some masterful plan, I had simply been... lucky. That's when the shakes really kicked in; it was almost more than I could do to manage the motorcycle.

Luckily, the shakes slowed after about ten minutes. John signaled for us to pull off the road and camp for the night. I made some passing comment about vibrations from the bike; looking back now, I doubt I fooled him. A little later, that notion was confirmed for me.

CHAPTER FIFTEEN

We had set up camp and secured everything for the night. After the meal preparation, John put on a pot of coffee and lit a cigar. I have no memory of what we ate. John seemed at peace with what had happened. As we sat around the campfire later, I felt completely exhausted. I couldn't stop yawning, and each time I did, I shook my head trying to wake up.

"Paul," Rourke said softly, "you're experiencing what is called adrenal let-down. It is natural after what you went through back there. Fear and physical activity, particularly when combined kick in the adrenal gland and floods your body with adrenalin. Adrenalin gives you extra strength and speed, numbs the body to minor injuries, and lets you function at a higher level."

"It is very much like taking amphetamine; in fact, the military did a lot of experimenting during World War II with amphetamines. They gave them to aircrews and special combat units to enhance performance during long and hazardous missions. The problem is the 'crash' afterwards. That's what you're experiencing right now, the 'crash' or medically speaking, the adrenal let-down. Go to sleep; you'll feel better in the morning. I'll stand watch tonight. If you wake up, you can relieve me."

I did as he suggested and about three hours later, I woke up and felt more like my old self. John went to sleep and I dissected my day and my feelings. It was a very long night for me. John woke up a few hours later, stoked the fire back to life, and warmed up a small pot of coffee; we were nearly out of the leftover coffee we took as part of our provisions from the plane. We didn't talk much that morning. John apparently didn't have anything to say, and I, well—I hadn't figured out what to say yet. Forty-five minutes later, we poured the remnants on the fire, covered it with dirt, and stirred. Then, we emptied our bladders on the remains and mounted the bikes heading east—always east.

My Reflections:

These few pages... Reading them again I'm struck with what happened, how fast it happened and the long term impact it was having on me. That doesn't come across very well in these few pages and I'm sorry. The truth is things were happening too quickly. There was too much to try and absorb, and precious little time to even think.

My world shattered and like a broken mirror, it couldn't be put back together... Nor could I deal with it all. Things, like I said, were simply coming at me from every direction, one right after the other. It wasn't that I couldn't think, I didn't think. I acted and I reacted, there was no time to do anything else.

When John and I were on the Harleys I tried to think; but it wasn't the kind of thinking that gives you direction or peace as you try to analyze and problem solve. My only imperative was to stay alive; just one more day, just for one more mile, just to the next sunrise and then to the next sunset. Around the campfires, my body was getting stronger, leaner. My mind was able to function in areas that had never even been a consideration for me. My heart was staggered and my soul... I didn't know about my soul at this juncture. There were questions I had no answers for because I often did not realize the questions had not been asked, yet!

PART II

MY VIEW OF THE NIGHTMARE BEGINNING

CHAPTER SIXTEEN

To be honest, the next several days remain pretty much a blur to me. In that short span of time, a lot happened. During the few "down times" we had, usually when we parked the bikes and camped for the night, I was receiving information from and about John. He was trying to teach me, but there was just so much information. Luckily, my mind was opening up and I was able to absorb a lot.

I remember asking John, "Of all those bikes back there at the crash site, why did you take that particular one?"

"Couple of reasons," he said, his voice low. "I like Harleys; I already have a Low Rider like this," he affectionately patted the fuel tank between his legs, "back at the survival Retreat. It's about the best combination going for off-road and road use—good enough on gas, fast, handles well, lets you ride comfortably. I like it, I guess," he concluded.

"You've got reasons for everything, haven't you John?" He just smiled. "What are we doing John? Are we seeking revenge, are we avenging... are we dealing out vengeance? These words are all similar, yet they are different. What are we doing?"

He thought for a moment and said, "I can't speak for you Paul. For me it is pretty simple. We are trying to survive and for me I'm seeking..." He paused. "I'm seeking justice."

CHAPTER SEVENTEEN

There was the time when it looked to me like John had almost driven past an abandoned truck, but then skidded the Harley into a tight left and said we needed to go check out the truck trailer. This is where our next "sticky wicket" started and it would serve as a forecast for the next several days. "Common carrier," he said softly. "Abandoned. After we run the Geiger counter over it, we can check what's inside—might be something useful. Shut off your bike. I don't think we're gonna find any gas here."

What we had found was a resupply point; there was even an unopened package of coffee under the front seat of the truck. We loaded up on ammo; we had found some .45, .357 Magnum, .308 and .223, and some terrible tasting baby food. It was about then we were discovered by Captain Nelson Pincham of the Texas Independent Paramilitary Response Group who tried to "arrest" us as looters. That plan didn't go well for the Captain. When ordered to surrender his guns to the Captain, John executed a move called the road-agent spin and sent the paramilitaries, better known as paramils, down the road, minus four dead troopers.

The Captain had told us there were more bands of paramilitaries roaming the countryside. They functioned somewhere between vigilantes and brigands; we would have more run-ins with them later on during the trip. As we approached El Paso, I heard gunfire. "What's all that shooting?" I asked John.

"Either some Mexicans are trying to get across the border into here, which would be damned foolish just now, or a pile of Americans are trying to get across into Mexico. This would be just the reverse of the usual situation, wouldn't it? White Anglo-Saxon Protestant wetbacks."

"Jees, you were right about this place. Everything looks like it's been looted fifty times," I told John as we got closer. The entire town had lost its mind and riots were fully in swing. I don't know how many we actually killed trying to get out of El Paso. Suffice it to say, El Paso was a nightmare of irrelevant violence and gratuitous death.

CHAPTER EIGHTEEN

Then two days later, we find HER on our way to Van Horn, Texas. What appeared to be the body of a woman was lying on the shoulder of the road. Slowing down, John said, "Wait here in case it's a trap of some kind."

"What do you mean—a trap?"

"Could be those paramilitary guys, could be anyone—put a woman's body down beside the road, and most people are going to stop, right? Plenty of cover back by those dunes, right?"

"Yeah, but she's awful still; hasn't moved since we spotted her."

"Could be dead already, maybe just a bag of rags stuffed into some old clothes. Keep me covered," John said, in a near whisper. He swung the CAR-15 across the front of the Harley and started the bike slowly across the road, throwing a glance back over his shoulder. I readied the German MP-40 subgun to back him up. Cutting a wide arc across the opposite shoulder and going off onto the sand, he ran a circle around the body.

I was close behind keeping a constant eye in all directions. Parking his Harley on the hard surface of the road, he dismounted and knelt to feel her pulse. He said it was weak, but steady; her skin was waxy-appearing and cold to the touch. "Shock." he called out. "Heat prostration. Paul—do a wide circle to make sure she doesn't have any friends, then come over—we've got to get her out of the sun."

When I returned, John and I carried her over to an outcropping of rocks where there was some shade. Even dirty and disheveled, she was incredibly beautiful. John studied her and said she looked familiar, "Somewhere in the back of my mind, I know I've seen the face before. I wouldn't forget her."

EVERYMAN

Over the next hours, she kept mumbling about a jeep. John surmised that if there was one out there, it should mean food and water, maybe gasoline. He left me guarding her and went to check. I sat in the darkness, watching the rising and falling of the strange girl's chest in the moonlight and listening to her heavy breathing; the Schmeisser cradled in my lap. She was beautiful. I'd given up cigarette smoking two years earlier, but now, having a cigarette was all I could think about.

According to the Timex on my wrist, John had been gone for more than an hour. When he returned, he said he had found her jeep with a bullet hole in the radiator and four dead men in the immediate vicinity; one with his throat slit, one dead by a martial arts blow that drove the bone from his broken nose up into his brain, and the remainder shot. John had also found a Walther P-38K. "A professional piece of hardware—the muzzle threaded on the inside for a silencer which I found inside one of the tubular supports for the seat frame," he explained.

It was several hours before she awoke. "What's that I smell?" Her voice was hoarse.

"Coffee," John said. "Want some? It's yours anyway."

She sat up, moving slowly then leaning back on her elbow. "Who are you?" she asked, her voice still not quite right-sounding.

"My name is John Rourke, he's Paul Rubenstein." She turned and I smiled and gave her a little salute.

"What the hell are you doing drinking my coffee?"

"Pleasant, aren't we?" John said. "You were dying and we saved your life. I went back and found your jeep, buried your boyfriend or husband a few miles back beyond that and then hauled up the gasoline, the water, the food, and some of your stuff. Then, so we didn't have to leave you alone and could make sure your fever didn't go up, we slept in shifts the rest of the night watching you. I figure that earns us a cup of coffee, some gas, and some food and water. Got any objections?"

"You got any cigarettes?" she said.

Rourke tossed a half-empty pack of cigarettes to her. "I guess these are yours—found 'em at the jeep." She started to reach out her left arm for the cigarettes and winced.

59

"You were shot in the forearm," John said then looked back to his coffee, sipping at it.

"Anybody got a light?" she asked.

John reached into his jeans and pulled out his Zippo, leaned across to her and working the wheel, the blue-yellow flame leaped up and flickered in the wind. The girl looked at him across it, their eyes meeting; then she bent her head, brushing the hair back.

"What happened?"

John explained that we had spotted her body by the side of the road, saw she was hurt, and tried to help.

"Did I talk—I mean how did you know where to find the jeep?"

"You didn't say much," Rourke said, adding, "Don't worry. You mumbled something about a jeep and something about Sam Chambers. If I remember, before the war, he was still down here in Texas—had just been appointed Secretary of Communications to the President; and, I think your name is Natalie."

"It is. What war?" she said.

"Don't you know about the war?" I asked, leaning toward her.

"What war?" she said.

CHAPTER NINETEEN

The next day, she was able to mount behind me on the Harley and we headed east again. Mid-morning, we came across a group of refugees from a town even John had never heard of. He looked over to me and said, "Tell them we don't mean them any harm." I guess I was the designated wussy looking member of the team that no one would be intimidated by. Their story was tragic; one woman was carrying the body of her dead baby. We did what we could for them. There had been a cafe and a U.S. Border Patrol Station in the town. The woman told us a band of brigands had come through. As she spoke, she was rocking back and forth on her knees on the ground, her dirty face tear-streaked with blood on the front of her dress from the dead infant she had carried through the night.

Natalie said, "They must be up ahead of us, somewhere."

"I hope we get to meet them," I said, my voice tightening with anger.

John looked at Natalie, then at me, then back at the refugees and said, "Chances are, we'll meet up with them. Anybody see who shot that woman's baby—what he looked like?"

Natalie had folded the woman in her arms. She suddenly stopped crying, looking up at John Rourke, saying, "I saw him. Not too tall, thin kind of, and had blonde hair, curly and pretty like a girl maybe, and this little beard on the end of his chin. Carried a long, fancy-lookin' pistol—that's what he used to kill my baby; that's what he killed her with."

John leaned forward to the woman, huddled there in Natalie's arms, saying slowly and deliberately, his voice almost a whisper, "I can't promise you we'll find that man, but I can promise you that if we do, I'll kill him for you." He started to turn away and caught Natalie's blue eyes staring at him. He didn't look away.

I think that was really the first time it hit me; there was an incredible amount of tension between these two. Sometimes it seemed like they hated each other. Other times they just distrusted each other, but there was something else I didn't identify then. Nope, that would come later.

Chapter Twenty

Natalie kept a four-barreled COP derringer-type pistol and the Walther. She gave the other guns John had salvaged from the jeep and the men she had killed, to the most likely-looking of the refugee group. The COP .357 was a four barrel .357 derringer style pistol that fired with a rotating striker. John told me it had been designed by a guy name Robert Hillberg and was made by COP, Inc. from Torrance, California.

As we drove away, Natalie turned to watch as the refugees went on their way, probably to nowhere. That night as we sat around the campfire, I learned that John's primary handguns are fairly unique; his Detonics pistols were innovations, not just a cut down version of a full-sized 1911. They were combat .45 semi-automatic pistols. An engineer with the Explosives Corporation of America named Pat Yates, and a former Office of Special Services operative named Sid Woodcock, had worked on the original prototypes for the CombatMaster before Mike Maes, a manager with EXCOA and Sid Woodcock had "formalized their collaborative work."

I really did not understand exactly what that meant and John did not elaborate much. He just put it down to "Any time you create something this innovative, this new... you have to make sure all the legal nuisances are taken care of before you go public with a project."

In any event, apparently that freed Yates to fully develop his compact 1911 design. Over the course of a few years, the CombatMaster was developed, tested, and put into production in 1976, and the rest as they say, was history. I was actually becoming fairly conversant in an area I never thought I could learn; firearms.

CHAPTER TWENTY-ONE

We headed out for Van Horn about seventy-five miles away. This was our next "sticky wicket." It was where we met one of our great tragedies and I almost died. John had sent me to reconnoiter the town. Luckily, I was moving slowly on the Harley because I never saw the wire that snatched me off the bike, slamming me hard onto the pavement and knocking the breath out of me. The next thing I knew, I was being pummeled by four young men with clubs; I never had a chance.

Thirty minutes later, John came around a corner on his bike and saw me on my knees at the end of the street. My captors were teenagers, high school age. They had tied my hands and arms stretched between the rear axle of an overturned truck and a support column for one of the smaller factory loading docks. There was a young man standing beside me holding an assault rifle with a fixed bayonet pointed at the side of my throat. Surrounding us was a group of teenagers, armed with everything from old shotguns to axes. I screamed, "John, go back!" The guy shoved the bayonet harder against my throat, and I shut up.

John dismounted and tried to talk our way out of the situation. He was able to determine that these kids had been away on a senior class field trip when the nukes had fallen. Their bus ran out of gas and by the time they had walked back, everyone in town was gone. They knew where some guns were located, and they had been running the town ever since. They knew they had radiation sickness and that they were all dying, but they were guarding the town until their families got back. Not only did they have radiation poisoning but they were lost souls, desperately trying to make sanity out of an insane world. It was like they were all mad. I was still tied up and waiting to get my throat sliced or shot out. Within just a few minutes, it became clear that the dialog was proving unproductive and the kids were escalating toward an increasing threat.

Seeing no other chance, John pulled the trigger on the CAR-15 twice, cutting down the young man with the bayonet just as he started to stab me with it. Gunfire erupted on the street and when it was over, I looked up at John shouting, "They're only kids, John!"

It had been a slaughter; all of the kids went down. I had to remember they had been ready to slaughter us; even that didn't help much. Damn the choices we had to make. Rourke, his eyes hard, bit his lower lip then shouted, "God help me; I know that, damnit! Paul, they knew they were dying; they just forced us to help them in the process. Remember, the first one I shot was about to kill you," he said, shaking with rage.

It took several minutes for him to regain control and in the process, John somehow remembered. He turned to Natalie and said, "I saw you in South America, a few years ago. You were a blonde—I think your eyes were green, but it was you. Contact lenses?" He then looked up at the girl, taking off his sunglasses and pushing them back past his forehead into his hair. He squinted past the midday sun at her.

"They were contact lenses," she nodded, "but what now?"

"You mean about this or about me remembering you?" John asked softly.

"Whatever," the girl said.

"Let's stick to this for now—we can worry about the other thing later. We still need supplies."

I was losing it, "I can't understand this!" I said, almost crying.

"What?" Rourke asked.

"We just killed ten perfectly decent kids, or at least they were. What's happening?"

"Sometimes when people realize they're dying, it's almost as if they step out of themselves," John said. "Those kids were smart enough to realize what was happening to them and they focused their energies, their thoughts—everything—on guarding this town. Kind of calculated mass hysteria. It didn't matter to them that it was wholly irrational, impossible, or even that they knew I was right and no one was coming back here for them. Probably once the first one started noticing what was happening and then some of the others started coming up with the symptoms, they just made a sort of pact. Kids are big on that sort of thing—pacts, blood oaths." The town of Van Horn, Texas, by all accounts, died that day.

65

We found another resupply opportunity in a warehouse. We stocked up on food, gas, and water. I found some cigars for John and some cigarettes for Natalie. John tried to offer a suggestion on what had happened here. "The way I've got it figured, everybody in the town just evacuated—I don't know to where. Then, those kids returned and tried to guard the place. Looks like they did a pretty good job; I'd guess the lead elements of the brigand force probably pulled in there, got killed, and never reported back."

"Then they're still ahead of us," the girl stated, more than asked.

"Yeah—strong and probably by now spoiling for a good fight. I wouldn't worry. We're bound to bump into them," Rourke concluded.

We had taken comparatively little. I resealed the door just in case the original owner was still alive and might return. We found a light blue pickup truck a half-hour earlier and, with the added supplies, decided on taking it along—the keys had been in it. The most awkward thing had been getting the Harleys aboard the truck and securing them. We drove in silence; I began to whistle occasionally, some lonely-sounding tune I couldn't recall the name of.

Finally, John pulled over and we set up camp. The mood was somber to say the least. "Hey," I said, trying to lighten up the situation, afraid things were going to go too far. "Why don't we all have a drink? I mean, I could use one—we got six bottles back in the truck. Where'd you put 'em, John?"

"In the front right hand corner," Rourke answered, not looking at me, but looking at the dark-haired, blue-eyed girl instead, her face glowing in the warm light of the lantern. "There, just in front of my bike, I wrapped 'em up in an old towel I found. Go get one if you want."

Afterwards, I passed the bottle around—Seagram's Seven. John took a hard pull on it, leaning back on the pickup's rear bumper. He looked at the girl as she drank. When she handed the bottle back to me she asked him, "Have you remembered me yet?"

She just shook her head, the same gesture of brushing her hair from her face, making Rourke see her again as she had been years earlier, as he remembered her. She took another drink, and so did I. John alternately watched the stars overhead and stared at his watch, only once more taking a drink.

Between the new demands I was putting on my body and my indulgence on Seagrams Seven, I passed out, the bottle beside me more than half-empty.

John told me the rest of the evening's story the next day. "I must trust you," the girl said, standing up, weaving a bit as she walked around the lantern, and then sitting down on the ground beside him.

"Why do you say that?" he asked as she picked up the bottle and drank from it.

"I trust—trust you because otherwise I wouldn't let myself get drunk around you! You will have to promise me," she whispered, leaning toward him and smiling, "that if I start to talk, you won't listen—I mean, if I say anything personal or like that."

He told me that's when she leaned toward him and kissed him on the mouth. "There, Mister Goody-goody," she laughed. "That didn't hurt, did it?"

He whispered, "No—it didn't hurt. The problem is it felt too good." He dropped the cigar butt on the ground and kicked it out with the heel of his boot, folding the girl into his left arm and letting her head sink against his chest.

Later, he told me, "In that moment, I could hear her breathing, slow and even against me. I looked up at the stars; the warmth of the woman in my arms only heightening the loneliness, and I wondered what was in the stars—was there another world where men and women hadn't been foolish enough to destroy everything as it was now destroyed here. As the girl stirred against me, I closed my eyes. Her breathing, its evenness, and the warmth of her body in the desert cold... I opened my eyes and stared down at her in the light of the lamp. I eased her head down onto the rolled-up blanket beside me and stood up to put out the lantern. I'm a man who has always screamed inwardly, silently, and this time, I screamed the name 'Sarah!'"

CHAPTER TWENTY-TWO

The next day John left early; he went searching. When he returned, he drove up the grade into the sheltered campsite where the truck was parked and spotted me sitting by the Coleman stove with a cup of coffee in both hands. Natalie was standing by the front of the truck, and all Rourke could see of her as he eased the bike to a halt was her back. I had a hell of a hangover; I told John, "Shut off the motor… my head is…"

He laughed, killed the Harley engine, and walked over. He dropped to a crouch next to me, pouring himself some coffee, and asked, "What's with her?"

"What? Oh—I don't know—she's been that way ever since she woke up and found you were gone," I said, my voice shaky.

"So, what did you find out, Rourke?" He looked up; she had hands on her hips, feet a little apart, tiny chin jutted forward with fixed eyes staring at him.

"You look cheerful this morning," he said. "What I found out was that the paramilitary is a few hours behind us with a large force. The brigands are a few hours ahead of us with a large force, even larger than the paramils. If we meet up with the paramils, we've had it. Paul and I had a run-in with one of their patrols before we bumped into you."

"The officer who commanded the patrol is with the paramil force I saw," he continued. "He'll spot us, we'll get shot—and probably you too since you're with us. They're southwest of us now heading northeast along the road. The brigands were heading southwest. For a while I thought they'd run into the paramils, but then they turned off into the desert. Probably going to be staying in this area for a while."

John estimated the force at close to 350 men. They traveled in trucks and jeeps in a ragged wedge formation along the road with outriders on dirt bikes paralleling their movements and working back and forth, up and down the convoy line like herders moving cattle or sheep. He judged they were making approximately fifty miles per hour and with their numbers, there was no reason to suppose they wouldn't press on for fourteen or more hours per day—as long as daylight lasted.

Miles after that and from another overlook, he told us that he had watched the road below and saw the brigands. There were more than two dozen long-haul eighteen-wheeler trucks at their center, traveling four abreast and consuming the entire highway space with squads of motorcycle riders in front and in back and on the shoulders, all heavily armed. He judged the strength of the brigand force at better than 400 men and women. For some reason, they were heading back in the direction of Van Horn at about fifty miles per hour. The brigand column changed directions, moving into a long, single column and heading into the desert. That would have put the brigands ahead of us and the paramilitary force behind us.

Even with a hangover, I saw we were in trouble. We couldn't go southwest; we would run into the paramils, and now, we had brigands to deal with. We were "between a rock and a hard spot" and "caught on the horns of a dilemma." John determined our only course of action was to try and hook up with the brigands, "The paramils will kill us on sight."

That would prove easier said than done. Once we made contact with the brigands, John was forced to fight their leader, a big burly man named Mike and four of his henchmen. Mike's second-in-command, a pale blue–eyed baby faced killer name Deke, challenged Rourke to a shootout. Deke was a slim, blonde-haired man with a little imperial on his chin who wore a cut-away Hollywood-style fast-draw rig with a glinting, nickel-plated single-action revolver; the hammer spur built up, the butt canted rearward, the muzzle forward on his right hip, and a heavy leather glove on his left hand. Rourke had done some competitive fast-draw and had good friends who competed in the sport. He knew the light-speed draws a trained fast-draw man could make.

"I've seen that kind of shooting before," Natalie said, as we stood next to the truck.

"So have I," Rourke said softly, looking into her blue eyes. "He holds his hand on the gun butt, his left hand edged in front of the holster. On the signal, he rocks the gun out of the leather; the hand with the glove slaps the hammer back, fans it, and the gun goes off. I think he probably has the trigger tied back, so he doesn't even have to bother touching it."

"He probably does," the girl said. "You want this?" she asked, gesturing toward the Python still slung diagonally across her body.

"No—I'll use these," he said, reaching into the cab of the truck and taking the double shoulder rig and the .45s. He put his arms into the shoulder harness and raised the harness up over his head, letting it drop to his shoulders and then he settled the holsters comfortably in place. He snatched the gun from the holster under his left armpit, loaded it to his satisfaction, worked the slide several times, and then locked the slide back, reinserting the magazine and letting the slide stop down. He raised the thumb safety, leaving the pistol cocked and locked; then, he settled it back into the holster, closing the snaps for the trigger guard speed break. Then he did the same thing on the gun under his right arm; the girl looked up at him, her eyes hard, her jaw set. "You're crazy—you can't match that kind of speed with a conventional gun."

"These aren't conventional guns," Rourke told her as he walked to the gun fight. I followed; hell, the world had disintegrated to the point where I was about to witness an Old West shoot out. My head was spinning out of control, just like my world was. They stood still facing each other like something out of an old movie. Then, it happened.

Deke's six-gun was out, his left hand streaking back fast, the big revolver belching fire and roaring like a grenade going off near his ears. Rourke hit the mud and rolled, the Detonics in his right hand firing once, then once again, the first round thudding into Deke's midsection, punching through the arm and into the blonde-haired man's gut. Deke wheeled, dropping to one knee; Rourke's second shot impacted into Deke's chest as the single-action fired, the bullet spitting into the mud less than three feet in front of him.

That's when Rourke fired a third time, the jacketed hollow point punching into Deke's head, almost dead-square between the eyes. Rourke stood in the heavy rain now washing around him in a torrent. We both moved beside him. Rourke edged the body over with the toe of his boot. The blue eyes were wide open, the head cracked up the forehead—the eyes were just staring though as the rain fell against them. Rourke could do nothing but stare down into them himself. He had kept his promise to the woman with the dead infant.

CHAPTER TWENTY-THREE

When things settled down, one of the brigand women came up to John as we stood together and said, "Hey—whatever your name is."

"John Rourke," he'd told her.

"Well—John Rourke—listen. I'm going to do you a good turn—there's a kind of rule around here—any snatch that ain't claimed at night is open property for anyone in the camp. So, you or the little guy had better be sleepin' with that chick you brought in with you, or you're gonna have a fight on your hands. There's almost twice as many guys as there's women around for 'em. You get what I mean?" Rourke nodded; the brigands broke camp and, after a few hours of driving, set up for the evening in the pouring rain.

"What do we do now?" I asked.

"Well, we can't sleep, cook, and live inside the cab here, "Rourke said. "You and I will take some of those ground clothes we've been using and run a canopy out from the rear bed of the truck—we can sleep... maybe in the truck bed. After we cover the bikes and everything, it should be pretty dry back there." Then turning to Natalie, Rourke said, "And you can keep an eye peeled while Rubenstein and I get the shelter up—huh? And stay dry."

"I can do my share of the work," she said angrily. Later, we sat in relative silence, all three of us exhausted from the ordeal of the day. At Rourke's suggestion, I broke out another bottle of the whiskey, and we drank, but only moderately. Finally, with the shelter flap partially open for ventilation, we sat beside its edge staring out into the rain. I asked, "John—what are we gonna do now? It looks like they'll be setting up for a battle as soon as the rain slacks up."

Rourke sighed heavily, lighting one of his cigars and holding the flame of the Zippo for Natalie's cigarette. "The paramils won't be moving far in this weather—

they looked less prepared for rough weather than the brigands did. I don't think we're gonna see much before this lets up, probably not for several hours afterwards. I could be wrong. I'd imagine if Mike's awake, he's putting out guards by that road, just in case. Depends on how tough the paramils are."

"We gonna try and get out?" I asked. "The paramils aren't good guys."

"Well, I admit we had a kind of bad experience with them. But somebody's gotta go up against the brigands, and it doesn't look like there's any kind of government left," John said.

"What do you think is left?" I queried, taking off my glasses and rubbing my eyes.

"Probably more of Russia than there is of us," Rourke said, glancing toward the girl. "But I don't know for certain. Looks like a good deal of the country is going to be uninhabitable for a long time. Look at this weather we're having too. It's supposed to be hot out there, but I bet the temperature is pushing down to 40 or so. You notice the sunsets? Each night, they've been a little redder. All that crap from the bomb blasts is getting up into the atmosphere and staying there."

"You mean, we're all gonna die?"

As John started to answer me, Natalie cut in, saying, "No—listen. Just trust me because I know something about this. The radiation couldn't have done that much damage. The world is going to survive—I just know it."

Rourke looked at her saying, "I know you know it."

I started getting up. "What do you mean?

"Sit down and relax Paul," Rourke commanded me in his voice low.

The girl sighed heavily, snapping the butt of her cigarette through the opening in the shelter flap and into the mud outside. "He means I'm Russian."

"Russian!" I shouted.

"She's one of the top women in the KGB—the Committee for State Security—the Russian version of the CIA and FBI rolled into one," Rourke said, exhaling a cloud of the gray cigar smoke.

"What—you!" and I started toward her, angry and hurt, not knowing exactly what I was going to do but John's left hand shot out, pushing against my chest and knocking me back against the truck bed. Rourke glanced down. The medium-frame, four-barreled COP derringer pistol was in her right hand.

Her voice was trembling as she rasped, "Please Paul—I don't want to use this, please?"

"What do you mean?" I said. "You mean after all we've been through together, after the way you lied to us? We saved your life, lady!"

"I didn't ask you to come along and find me. I don't mean any harm to either of you—I almost love you both—please, Paul!"

I started to get to my feet. Rourke— almost in one motion—pushed me back again and twisted the COP pistol out of the girl's hand, saying, "Now both of you—knock it off!"

"Knock it off," I said, my lips drawn back in a strange mixture of incredulity and anger. I pushed the glasses off the bridge of my nose and said, "It's not enough that the Russians have destroyed the world practically, but they killed millions of Americans—yeah, knock it off! What about you, John? You gonna knock it off? Just because you miss your wife and you think maybe she's dead and... this one comes along and... she is a knockout and she is hot for you to get into her pants... What—you think I'm blind? She's a goddamned communist agent, John!" I was shouting.

"I didn't drop any bombs; I didn't give any attack orders, Paul! Leave me alone!" The girl nervously pulled another cigarette from the pack and tried lighting a match, but her hand was shaking so badly the matches kept breaking.

John lit her cigarette and leaned back, closing the lighter, saying, "He's right; you're right. You didn't drop any bombs—you were just being a patriotic Russian. And now, you're here in this country and you're looking for Samuel Chambers. Why? To kill him? To keep him from serving as a rallying point for the resistance? Right?"

"I'm just doing my damned job, John. It's my job!"

"I had a job like that once," John told her, "but you know what I did? I quit. That's where you remembered me from—South America, a few years ago. I was down there a lot in those days. I didn't quit because my philosophy changed or anything—I just quit because I wanted to and figured I'd done my time. You could do the same, couldn't you?"

"I've got other reasons," she said, staring into the cigarette in her right hand. "I believe in what I'm doing."

"You didn't see your face when you looked at those refugees, the woman with the dead baby. You're on the wrong side," he told her.

"Is that why you didn't try and kill me when you recognized me?" she asked, looking up at him.

"No—that isn't why," he answered.

"How long have you known, John?" I asked.

"Long enough—after the first couple of days, I was sure." Then turning to the girl, he said, "Is Karamatsov here too? You always worked with him down south."

The girl said nothing for a long moment, then, "Yes."

"Who the hell is Karamatsov?" I asked, leaning forward.

Rourke started to answer but the girl cut him off, her voice suddenly lifeless-sounding, "He's the best agent in the KGB—at least he thinks so, and everyone tells him that. He's—I guess it doesn't matter—he's in charge of the newly formed American branch of the KGB—he's the top man in your entire country. The only man who can overrule him here is General Varakov—he's the military commander for the North American Army of Occupation."

"This is like some kind of a nightmare," I said as I took off my glasses and stared out into the rain. "During World War II, my aunt was trapped over in Germany when the war broke out. They found out she was Jewish and they arrested her; we never heard from her again. I grew up hating the Nazis for what they'd done. What the hell do you think American kids are gonna grow up hating, Natalie? Huh? How many houses and apartment buildings and farms—schools, office buildings . . . how many places just stopped existing? How many children and women and little dogs and cats and everything else that matters in life did you people kill that night? Jees—you guys make Hitler look like some kinda bush leaguer!"

She told me this is was war and she had no choice. "The U.S. ultimatum in Afghanistan, there was no choice, Paul—no choice. We had to strike first! And then, your own president held back U.S. retaliation until the last possible minute—we didn't know!"

Nothing made sense to me. My world had been destroyed, my universe changed and my damn life was sent spinning off at an angle... by a damn mistake, by a miscalculation, by an accident. What the hell kind of celestial joke had been played on us? More than being stunned... I was madder than hell. It was almost a rage, but more complicated than that simple emotion. I felt betrayal; betrayal from the world, I knew... betrayal from Natalie... betrayal from... hell, from history and even God himself. Were we, the Jews of the world destined to go through another holocaust?

I found myself having been drawn to Natalie's beauty and at the same time, moments ago I had wanted to kill her. Not her so much as kill everything she stood for; everything the Night of the War had created. I wanted to kill everything and everyone that had a part in it. I had trusted Natalie and now she was the focus of my rage.

Intellectually, I knew she was as much a pawn of the universe as Rourke and I. Emotionally... I raged. Against her, the Russians; against the war. Honestly, I raged against God for allowing all of this to even occur.

CHAPTER TWENTY-FOUR

"Listen to us," Rourke said. "Things haven't changed at all since the war, have they?" He closed his eyes and leaned his head back against the edge of the pickup's tailgate.

No one spoke for a while, and all I could hear was the unseasonably heavy rain. I elected to sleep in the bed of the pickup truck, curled up with the bikes and most of our gear, trying to make sense of this new situation and needing time alone to calm myself down. A fight was probably in the cards tomorrow between brigands and the paramils; and, somehow I knew that at least for the moment, all concentration should be directed towards our survival—all three of us.

John told me the next day that he and Natalie were lying beside one another under the tarps, listening to the rain, when one of the brigands passed by. He stuck his head under the shelter flap, then seeing Rourke and the girl together, he grunted, "Sorry, man—I didn't know if—see ya," then walked away. Rourke had one of the Detonics pistols under the blanket, the hammer cocked, and the safety down with his finger against the trigger.

After the man had gone and Rourke lowered the hammer on the pistol; the girl started to cry. Rourke heard the strange sound from her before he turned and saw the tears. Then, he asked her why. "He's right—what we did," she whispered, her voice catching in her throat.

"Yes, Paul is right," Rourke said. "But if everybody who isn't Russian winds up hating everybody who is Russian, what's that gonna do, huh?"

"What kind of man are you? He was right, he was right, you know," the girl said to him. "I did try everything I could to get you to come after me—I guess I still am. What? Was it because you knew who I was, thought I was Karamatsov's woman or something?"

"That didn't really have anything to do with it," he said then fell silent. The girl spoke again.

"Why then?"

"Why then what?" Rourke said, not turning to look at her.

"What we were saying before, that you didn't care I was a Russian agent, that I might be Karamatsov's woman. Why then?"

"Forget it," Rourke whispered. "You'll wake the kids." I guess he pointed up toward the truck bed, listening to me snore. I'm sure I gave my usual good performance.

"I won't forget it," she said. "Is it that wife you have, the one who's maybe still alive? What are you afraid of, you'll stop trying to find her?"

"No—I won't stop," he said. "Give me one of your cigarettes, I don't want to smell up the place."

She fumbled in the pocket of her jacket and handed Rourke the half-empty pack. Then she took it back, extracted one of the cigarettes, and lit it—her hands steady, the match lighting the first time. She inhaled hard then passed the cigarette over to Rourke. He stayed on his back, the cigarette in his lips, staring up at the top of the shelter and the darkness there.

"Is it that you'd be unfaithful to her?" she said, her voice barely above a whisper.

"Somethin' like that," Rourke said, snapping ashes from the tip of the cigarette out the partially open flap and into the rain.

"But—what if she isn't—" and the girl left the question unfinished.

"Then, it wouldn't be somethin' like that," Rourke said quietly, dragging hard on the cigarette then tossing it out into the rain. He could feel the girl moving beside him under the blanket.

"Are you human?" she whispered to him. He turned his head and looked at her and then without getting up, reached out his left hand and knotted his fingers into the dark hair at the nape of her neck, drawing her face down to him, looking for her eyes by the dim light there through the shelter flap. All he could see was shadow. He could feel her breath against his face, hear her breathing, and feel the pulse in her neck as he held her.

Her lips felt moist and warm against his cheek as she moved against him. Rourke took her face in his hands, found her mouth in the darkness and kissed her;

her breath was hot now and almost something he could taste, sweet, the release of her body against him being something he could feel in her as well as himself. She lay in his arms, and he could hear her whispering, "You are human."

Rourke touched his lips to hers again and heard her say, "Nothing is going to happen, is it John?"

"I don't know—go to sleep, huh? At least for now." He felt her head sink against his chest, and she whispered something he didn't hear.

CHAPTER TWENTY-FIVE

It was three A.M., and she was still sleeping in John's arms when I heard gunfire—single shots followed by a long series of shots—submachine gunfire, light like a 9mm would make. John said, "The damned fool paramils—it's a blasted night attack. Damn them!"

I started taking the shelter down and got the truck ready to roll. John hollered, "Mortars!" and dove onto me and Natalie, knocking us to the floor. The shelter trembled, the ground trembled, and the blast of the mortar was deafening.

John saw the brigand leader trembling in the cold, the riot shotgun in his hands. John suggested taking about fifty or seventy-five men, in two groups, down both sides of the road—right now. John offered to lead one group of men.

Then Natalie said, "Wait a minute; shhh, I hear something."

I looked skyward, saying, "Yeah—so do I, John. Listen."

"Helicopters—big ones and a lot of them—the paramils don't have that kind of equipment," John said and suddenly the entire campsite, the whole upper surface of the plateau, was bathed in powerful white light. A voice came across on a loudspeaker strapped to the chopper's left landing gear, "In the name of the Soviet People and the Soviet Army of Occupation, you are ordered to cease all hostilities on the ground. You are outnumbered by an armed force vastly superior to you—lay down your arms and stay where you are."

I muttered something to the effect of, "You can all go to hell!" and cranked up the "Schmeisser." John grabbed Natalie, forcing her down into the mud, the roar of heavy machine gunfire belching out of the darkness above me. Suddenly, I was hit in the stomach; I crumpled to the mud, the SMG in my hands still firing as I went down.

One second I felt like John Wayne in the Sands of Iwo Jima; the next second like a burning 2x4 hit me in the stomach. I couldn't move, couldn't breathe, and couldn't speak. In fact, the last of my senses that functioned before I passed out was hearing. The voice from the helicopters shouted over the speaker system again, "No one will move! Lay down your arms and surrender or you will be killed!"

John told me that while I was passed out, two of their helicopters landed on the plateau, while others hovered overhead, their floodlights illuminating the rain-soaked ground.

Natalie had disappeared in the confusion but she returned. When she did, she held a Kalashnikov pattern assault rifle in her right hand and had a Soviet officer and two enlisted men with her. "John," she said, "I've identified myself to the commander, Captain Machenkov. I had to tell him both of you were my prisoners, but don't worry. I'll straighten everything out with Karamatsov. Paul will get the best medical care we can give him, and you and Paul and I will be flown out of here in a few minutes to Galveston where we have a small base already operational. I know there's a field hospital there and between what you can do and our own doctors, I know Paul will be all right. Don't worry."

"What now?" Rourke asked her.

She advised John that she'd have to take his guns, the .45s. He was not in favor of that. She explained, "I told them you were my prisoners, but you have saved my life; because of the situation here on the ground, I'd let you remain armed. It was the best thing I could think of—they don't speak English. This officer is a doctor. John, please don't try anything. I know you, remember. And I promised everything will be all right. After Paul is well, you and Paul can leave—with your weapons and everything. I've even arranged for your motorcycles to be taken along."

John whispered to her, asking if she really believed them.

She responded saying, "Karamatsov is my husband, John—I really believe you'll go free. He'll do as I ask."

"Mrs. Karamatsov, huh? Any kids?"

"Don't be funny," she snapped. "No one knows about it—except for you now."

CHAPTER TWENTY-SIX

When I came to, much later, John related the conversation he had with our captors and the events that transpired while I was in surgery. Vladimir Karamatsov had stood behind the desk for a moment, smiling, then sat down, saying, "So—I understand you saved Natalia's life—you and the injured one — Rubenstein. He's a Jew, isn't he?"

"Natalia huh, not Natalie; I thought you were a communist, not a Nazi?" John said, looking at the woman.

"We have found Jews to be troublemakers in the past—I was only curious. We, as yet, have located nothing about him in our data banks. He is new to your agency?"

"He is not with the agency; we partnered up to survive," John said, but Karamatsov took little note.

John found out the American president had committed suicide rather than be taken captive; our new president was a guy name Samuel Chambers, and the Russians had captured him. John had been locked up, and it was several hours before he heard a knock on the door of the small two-bunk room he was locked in; the door opened and Natalia was standing there. She told John that I was out of surgery and in intensive care; she assured him I'd be fine. "No major damage to the intestines or whatever," she told him. "I don't know a lot about anatomy. They've got a tube in his stomach for drainage, but he's going to be all right."

"That's good," Rourke said. "Thanks—look, I know you tried. I'm not angry at you, really—you did what you could."

She hadn't said anything for a moment then said, "I saw Chambers—he's well. They haven't sedated him or anything. There's a plane coming from Chicago to pick you up—they'll want to take Chambers too. General Varakov wants to see you both. Actually, you're lucky—Varakov is a good man. He'll be easier than Vladimir would have been."

"Yeah, real lucky," Rourke said, not trying to disguise the bitterness in his voice.

"I brought you a cigar," she said. After a short talk, she hitched up the skirt over her right leg and pulled the COP pistol, the little stainless steel .357 Magnum from her right thigh, and pointed it at him. She stood up and walked to the door, smoothing her hair back from her face, tapping on the door, saying in Russian, "Corporal, come in here. This prisoner had a weapon—I've disarmed him. Come inside immediately and assist me."

The door opened and the young corporal said, "I will assist you, comrade captain," then stepped through the doorway. As he passed her, with the COP pistol clamped in her right fist, she straight-armed him in the right side of the neck. Rourke caught the young soldier before he hit the floor then eased him onto the bed. "How are you going to get out of this?" Rourke asked her.

"Don't worry about me. We can get Chambers freed and then get Paul out. I have already arranged for your motorcycles and equipment to be brought to one of the elevators they use for getting the planes up onto the field. There's a prop plane down there—it's fueled and flight checked. You can fly it?"

"Unless the gauges are in Arabic, yes. Why are you doing this?"

She looked at him, saying, "I gave my word—I keep my word, just like you do."

Chambers was being held just beyond the head of the stairs on the hospital wing, and Karamatsov's office was on the same floor. Their first stop was Samuel Chambers. After the president, they went for John's weapons—then they came for me. Natalia took me, complete with the I.V. and the stomach tube, from the hospital section and they loaded me aboard the plane. I can't say I remember much of the details of our escape; I was still pretty much sedated. That was good in that I didn't really feel the bumps and bangs associated with quick rescues on a fast-moving gurney. She volunteered to stay behind, convinced that Karamatsov would punish her, but not kill her. John's eyes locked onto Natalia's, and he wanted to say that he hoped he'd see her again. He wanted to kiss her good-bye, but he stuck out his right hand instead saying, "Good-bye."

After takeoff, John picked up the microphone. Chambers asked, "Who are you calling on the radio, Mr. Rourke?"

"I made a promise, Mr. President. I figure if you get on that frequency the paramils will call off the attack for you."

"Why should I?"

Quietly, Rourke said, "Mr. President—I gave my word I would; and with all due respect, this plane flies two ways: away from the Russians back there and right back toward them. Don't think I wouldn't! I gave my word that our air strike would be stopped in return for the Russians calling off a neutron weapon strike. Sounds like a pretty good deal to me. How about you?"

Handing Chambers the microphone, "You're on, sir," Rourke whispered in the darkness. He let out his breath when he heard the president begin to speak into the headset microphone. I missed all this excitement, catching up on my drug-induced beauty sleep instead. John landed the aircraft in east Texas where I was given additional medical aid and, in a couple of days, was pronounced fit enough for limited travel. John had used a twin engine plane to carry us across the Mississippi. There had been nothing below us. Once thriving cities were now obliterated; the course of the river itself even seemed altered. From the air, we saw no signs of life, and the vegetation that remained appeared to be dead or dying.

One of the troops at Chamber's headquarters had rigged the plane with a device similar to a Geiger counter that was a sensor which worked from outside of the craft. The radiation levels—if the device was accurate—were unbelievably high. John landed the plane just inside the Georgia line, what had been the Georgia line before, just below Chattanooga. The city was no longer really there—it had become a neutron bomb site. Neutron bombs were very "dirty" bombs. They did little physical destruction to standing structures; they simply killed people. The majority of the buildings were standing but there were no people at all, at least none who were still living.

Luckily, it was also uneventful, no shoot-outs. In Georgia, John left me with one of the bikes and the bulk of the supplies about fifty miles southeast of the Retreat. John talked a lot about the Retreat; honestly, it sounded too good to be true. He assured me it would be there and we'd be safe there. I just hoped we'd survive long enough to get there.

He said the trip the rest of the way would be hard going and could take another twelve hours. I told him I would be all right until he returned. He left the Steyr-Mannlicher SSG with me in a secure position in a high rock outcropping from which I could shoot if necessary. I had food, water, and blankets to keep me comfortable as well as pain medication if necessary. I knew this was something he had to do by himself; there was no telling what he would find, perhaps his family bloated and dead in their home.

The good news was President Chambers had shown him a map which afterwards Rourke had memorized then burned, but was still able to reproduce from memory. It showed strategic reserves of gasoline cached throughout the southeast; for our comparatively meager needs the supply was infinite.

I still wanted to go south to Florida to see if somehow my parents had survived. John told me I'd get the chance, but he hoped I would return. In a rare touching moment, he told me he counted only a few people as friends in life and I was one of these few; perhaps the only one left alive, though he supposed he should count the Russian girl, Natalia.

My Reflection:

My world was starting to fill back up. The threats had not lessened for us; and "us" now included the beautiful Russian spy Natalie, then later Natalia. Holy crap, Paul Rubenstein had met the President of the United States. He was riding motorcycles in high speed chases off road, he was being shot at and he was hit and almost died. He had seen death and he had caused death, but those things weren't really happening to me. They were happening to the other Paul. The one that was becoming; the one birthed in a plane crash and death.

It was me, my body, but I felt like I was standing outside myself watching the events of a movie unfolding before me. I was starting to feel a drop in my anxiety, a comfort starting to settle in. No, not comfort... the word would have to be confidence. For the first time in my life I had confidence IN ME!

I knew I trusted John, hell I didn't have a choice; however, had there been a choice, I would still trust him. There was even a glimmer of trust starting again where Natalia was concerned. John had a lifetime of experience in making split second, minute by minute life decisions. I hadn't; my decisions had been mundane, everyday stuff. Did I want cereal or a bagel for breakfast? Would I write about this story or that story? Was I finally going to marry Ruth or just keep things rolling along like always?

Conflict swirled over me with every realization of what I was feeling. Take Ruth; would it have been better to already have married her? Right now that was a big regret but, no sooner did I realize if I had, I would be searching for my wife instead of my fiancé. What exactly was the difference? I don't know, but it seemed there was one—somewhere.

Maybe all of the things in my life had actually turned out the way they should have. John had confidence in my abilities and was willing to teach me. Probably for the first time in my entire life, I was willing to be taught. For the first time in my life I had found true friendship; and I was willing to actually be a friend. I had a new definition of friendship developing. Not just a buddy to have drinks with; not just someone to have an "academic" conversation on life or philosophy. This was deeper; there was a bond I had never known that had simply sprang out of the ashes of the world I had known. I had someone I could trust to have my back and others trusted me to have their back... things I'd never had to consider before.

I was learning things, I was doing things... I was feeling things I had never experienced before. I truly did not know if I should be laughing or crying. So I drove that Harley, shot bad guys and stayed alive. The alternative didn't suit me.

PART III
ON OUR QUEST

CHAPTER TWENTY-SEVEN

While John was gone to explore the farm and to seek Sarah and the kids, I got hit by brigands. Luckily, they didn't attack me that first night, probably because they had no idea I was there. My wounds were still painful but on the mend. I was carrying the "Schmeisser" subgun, the Browning High Power, and John's own Steyr-Mannlicher SSG Special Rifle as companions. I was in the high rocks beyond the clearing where he had left me the previous day. Below me were perhaps a dozen figures, most of them men, but one or two possibly women. The figures—clearly brigands, heavily armed, dirty-looking, and out for blood—were slowly advancing up the rocks, firing to keep me pinned down until they could close in.

I figured I was going to die, Rourke was gone trying to find his family. I was alone with my "Schmeisser," the High Power and John's counter-sniper rifle. There would be a series of shots from the brigands to pin me down, then the brigands would advance; I would edge up and fire the green synthetic stocked rifle then duck down as the brigands shot again.

If the brigands had divided themselves into fire-and-maneuver elements, they could have swept over me easily; but fortunately, their tactics weren't that good. I was hurt but I was able to move, just not very fast or easily. Luckily, John had left me in a position with a good field of fire and some cover.

I lost count of the number of rounds I fired and the number of people I killed over the next few days. I just sighted and shot and then moved to a different position as dictated by the next threat I saw. My biggest fear was I would not see one of the bad guys before he drew a bead on me and I would die never knowing I was about to.

Then I got sight of John down below. *Thank God he made it back*, I thought as I watched him. Rourke had the CAR-15 across his back and was edging up the lip of the grade, hugging the pine trees and low rocks along the side and moving diagonally along the left flank of the attacking brigands. He climbed to the far end of the grade, looking down onto the flat expanse leading toward the high rocks. He could see me with the Steyr-Mannlicher SSG Special Rifle with the 3x9 scope at my shoulder; he waved then started firing and moving.

Between the bad guys I was able to polish off and the ones John took care of (some with his A.G. Russell Sting 1A boot knife and others with his CAR-15 and his Colt Python revolver) the gunfire eventually stopped. We had won this battle and were safe, at least for a while. John climbed to my vantage point when it was over.

He told me he had seen more brigands all over. In a low voice he said, "Gangs of them are everywhere." His eyes squinted behind the sunglasses against the bright morning sunlight. We sat watching the area below us for several minutes before he started telling me what had happened at his home.

"Edging along the boundary of the tree line, I could see the frame of the house was partially standing, like bleached bones of a dead thing, the walls burned and the house itself gone. I walked forward, hearing the howling of the dogs. The moon was full and I could see clearly. There wasn't a cloud in the sky; the stars were like a billion jewels in the velvet blanket of the sky."

He continued, "I stopped where the porch had been. Michael, my son, always liked to climb over the railing and I always told the boy to be careful. Annie, my daughter, had driven her tricycle into the railing once and knocked loose one of the finials, if that was what you called them. I remembered Sarah standing in the front door that morning after I had come back. She had taken me inside; we had had coffee and talked. She had shown me the drawings for her latest book and then we had gone upstairs to our room and made love. That room was gone, the bed, porch—probably even the coffee pot." John paused for a minute, remembering the scene. Unconsciously, he pulled out one of his thin dark cigars and that damned battered Zippo. When the cigar was finally lit, he inhaled deeply and let the smoke out slowly.

I sat and listened intently while keeping one eye out for more bad guys. Rourke was in a dark place, one unlike anything I had ever seen in him before. Frankly, I didn't know what to say to him. He sat next to me but mentally he was back at the farm, remembering... what, I didn't know yet. Honestly, I wasn't sure I wanted to know.

"The barn still stood," he continued, "the fire that gutted the house apparently had not spread. I circled the house twice and had found two things. First, the house had exploded and second, I found the charred and twisted frame of Annie's tricycle. I sat down on the ground and stared up at the stars, again wondering if there could be places where the things that called themselves intelligent life had elected to keep life rather than wantonly spoil it. I looked at the wreckage of the house behind me and decided there wasn't any intelligent life left. I started toward the barn then stopped, hearing something behind me."

He told me how four men, wild-looking, unshaven, hair long, and clothes torn, were coming toward him; one with a club, another with a knife almost as long as a sword, the third carrying a rock, and the fourth man with a gun. They were screaming something he couldn't understand and John fired at them with the CAR-15. The one with the rock went down followed by the man with the club. Then he fired at the man brandishing the knife, missing the man as he lunged toward him. Rourke rolled onto his back, snatching one of the stainless Detonics pistols into his right hand, the CAR-15 on the ground a yard away from him. As the man with the knife charged at him again, Rourke fired once, then once more.

Then there was the fourth of the wild men; the man with the gun and Rourke spun into a crouch, his eyes scanning the darkness. He heard a scream, like an animal dying then fell to the ground, rolled, and came up on his knees, the Detonics in both his fists, firing as the fourth man stormed toward him. The man's body lurched backwards and into the dirt. Rourke got to his feet and walked toward the man.

Rourke told me he realized the man was really little more than a boy. His beard was long in spots, but sparse; the hairline bowed still, the face underneath the beard looking to be a mass of acne-like sores. Rourke reached down for the gun—it was a reflex action with him. The pistol was old, European, and so battered and rusted that for a moment he couldn't identify it. The weight was wrong and he pointed the pistol to the ground and snapped the trigger.

There was a clicking sound, and Rourke said he looked up into the darkness, letting the gun fall to the ground from his hand. After a while, he reholstered his pistol and found the rifle on the ground. There was no thought of burying the four dead men. If he were to bury the dead, where would he start?

Mechanically, still half staring at the gutted frame of the house where his family had lived, he reloaded the Detonics and the CAR-15 with fresh magazines. He started away from the house then turned, remembering he'd been walking toward the barn before the attack. He opened the barn door; an owl fluttered in the darkness, the sound of the wings was too large for a bat. Rourke lit one of the angle head flashlights we had stolen that first night in Albuquerque.

John paused to take a puff of his thin black cigar, then continued telling how he scanned the barn floor, realizing the horses were gone and so was their tack. He walked toward the stalls and then remembered to flash the light behind him. He saw something catching the light. He walked toward the barn door, and then swung the door outward into the light of the stars and the moon.

He told me, "It was a sandwich bag, the kind Sarah had used for lunches she'd stash in the pocket of my jacket when I'd leave early in the mornings to go deer hunting." John told how he saw this bag nailed to the barn door and noticed something inside the bag and he ripped it off the nail. "It was a check," he told me, "the first two letters of the word 'Void' written across it—it was Sarah's writing. I turned the check over, shining the light on it and read:"

"My Dearest John, You were right. I don't know if you're still alive. I'm telling myself and the children that you survived. We are fine. The chickens died overnight but I don't think it was radiation. No one is sick. The Jenkins family came by and we're heading toward the mountains with them. I'm telling myself that you will find us. Maybe it will take a long time, but we won't give up hope. Don't you. The children love you. Annie has been good. Michael is more of a little man than we'd thought. Some thieves came by and Michael saved my life. We weren't hurt. Hurry. Always, Sarah."

"At the bottom," John said, "the letters were larger and scrawled quickly; I think it said, "I love you, John.""

Rourke took one last puff of his cigar and flicked the snub into the darkness. He continued the story, telling how he leaned back against the barn door, rereading the note, and when he was through, reread it again. He hadn't looked at his watch, but when finally he looked up, the moon seemed higher. He told me how he folded the half-voided check carefully and placed it in his wallet, looked up at the stars, and his voice barely a whisper said, "Thank you."

John explained how he slung the CAR-15 under his right shoulder and started walking away from the barn, past the gutted house, and into the woods. He stopped and looked back once, lit a cigar turned and didn't look back again. He then headed back to find me.

I tried to plumb the depth of the emotions he must be having. My thoughts were totally screwed up and swarming. If I could focus on John, maybe I could find some sanity outside of myself that would help me out of the quicksand I felt I was in. He knew they had lived; he did not know if they were alive. He knew they had survived the initial attack; he did not know if they would survive the aftermath. He knew they had left the farm; he did not know where they were. He knew he would search for them; he did not know if he would ever see them again. In the end, there was not much comfort or direction I could find for either of us.

Neither of us had control. Neither of us had a plan; we were simply searchers on a quest, a quest we probably would not survive. For me, the burning question was if we survived, if John found Sarah and the kids, if I found my parents, what great victories those would be. But what would happen next?

What would happen next? Would we find our families only to die together? *Well*, I decided, *that would be better than dying alone.* But in all honesty, I didn't know if it would be or not. Sleep came slowly to me that night, and my dreams were far from restful.

CHAPTER TWENTY-EIGHT

"Do you think they found your Retreat, John?" I asked, wondering if the brigands had located it before we had killed them.

He thought a moment then said, "No, that's the least of my worries. Maybe an archeologist will find it a thousand years from now but nobody's going to find it today, tomorrow, or twenty years from now. Trouble is..." Rourke paused and looked past me and beyond the rocks where the bodies of the brigands we had killed lay. "I wonder if twenty years from now I'm still going to be living in it."

"What do you mean, John?"

Rourke lit one of his small cigars, "What I mean, Paul, is the world. You look at the sunsets, the sunrises, the way the weather has been hot one day, cold the next, the rains, the winds. And if the world stays in one piece, what happens then? Can we rebuild? There are so many questions. Not enough of them have answers and the ones that do are tough answers."

"Paul," he said, "I don't know what I felt; hell, I don't know what I'm feelin' now."

I don't think I had ever seen a more tortured soul in my life. He told me he wanted to cry and he wanted to laugh, both at the same time. He was hurting. "Sarah. Michael. Annie. Alive. Maybe," he said. "At least they had survived the first strike."

Again, he held out the note Sarah had written then folded it tightly back into his wallet. Why, I wondered, did we both still carry a wallet, driver's license, and Social Security card? None of it mattered any more. Was it habit, just something we did out of rote memory, or was it an attempt to hold on to a little piece of normal, a little piece of sanity, a little piece of our old world?

He told me he was eager to begin searching for Sarah and the children; could Sarah and the children be somewhere in the mountains of northern Georgia? If so, he knew they would be hard to find. Were they somewhere else in Georgia, the Carolinas, or perhaps Tennessee? Every mile they traveled likely took them farther away, he realized, making the search just that much longer and more difficult. "Finding a woman and two children in a country full of refugees with the entire midsection of that country a radioactive desert with no law...then there's the Russians and the brigands and God only knows what else." He wiped his face with both hands, stood up and said, "Let's go."

CHAPTER TWENTY-NINE

We made our way back to the Harleys. John revved his bike, squinted against the sun and, using his combat-booted feet to support the machine rumbling between his legs, started it down the path. I followed as we made our way still closer to the Retreat.

"Sometimes," John said, "you get the feeling there's something happening; you don't know where or what, but that you're involved with it anyway and that someday you'll learn what it was and when. Sort of like the feeling you get when a shiver runs up your spine and people say that somebody's just walked across your grave. Maybe they have."

"What do you mean?" I asked, my voice sounding tired, about as tired as I felt.

"I don't know," Rourke told me, almost laughing. "Come on. Not much farther now." Rourke looked at me. I was exhausted; my wounds still depleted my strength. The road to the entrance of the Retreat was twisted and difficult. We rode the bikes, the engines barely above stalling, up the narrow pathway. Rourke eyed the familiar landmarks; he knew each tree and each rock. At least these things, for him, remained the same—unchanging.

CHAPTER THIRTY

"We're here," Rourke finally said.

As I looked around in all directions, the terrain looked exactly the same as it had moments ago; rocks and knurly pine trees with a thick layer of slick, brown needles that had fallen from the trees; and, an almost invisible path leading to the Retreat that only John could see. "Where?" I asked. "I don't see anything."

"You're not supposed to. Once I had the Retreat, I realized it would be useless to me if I couldn't absolutely rely on the fact that it wouldn't be discovered. That meant I had to have some sort of secret entrance. In comic books, movies, and science fiction, they put branches or shrubs in front of the cave entrance but none of that works. I wanted something more permanent."

"So what did you do?" I asked.

"Watch." Rourke dismounted the bike and walked toward the cracked and rough weathered granite wall before us. He looked down; we were approximately halfway up the mountainside. He walked to a large boulder to the right of his bike and then pushed against it with his hands. The boulder rolled away. He walked to his far left where a similar but squared-off rock butted against the granite face.

"See," Rourke said and began pushing on it. "This whole area of Georgia is built on a huge granite plate at varying depths. This mountain is an outcropping of it, extending all the way into Tennessee and maybe well beyond. I did a lot of research in archeology to come up with this—how the Egyptian tombs were sealed off, Mayan temples."

John braced himself against the rock and pushed it aside. There was rumbling in the rock itself and I drew back, unsure of what was happening next. The rock on which Rourke stood began to sink and, as it did, a slab of rock about the size of a single-car garage door began to slide inward. "Just weights and counterbalances,"

John said, smiling, his face reflected by the starlight. "When you want to open from inside, levers perform the same function as moving the rocks out here."

I leaned forward, peering into the gradually opening doorway and the darkness beyond. He motioned me to follow him. I did, into the darkness. I followed like an automaton, trusting in the knowledge that he knew where he was headed and I was too exhausted by now to even think on my own.

"Let's get the bikes inside," he said. We did and then he said, "Paul, there's a red-handled lever in there by the light switch. Swing it down and lock it under the notch."

"Got it, John," I answered less than enthusiastically, grabbing the lever and doing as he asked. He said nothing, but bent and rolled the two rock counterbalances into position and then stepped into the cave. He bent to the red-handled lever, loosed it safely from the notch retaining it and raised it; the granite doorway started to move, and the rock beneath us started shuddering audibly.

"Relax," he told me softly. He turned and saw me staring beyond at the edge of the red light to the steel double doors at the far end of the antechamber. "I've got ultrasonics installed to prevent insects or vermin from getting in—closed circuit TV up there," Rourke said, gesturing above our heads to the low stone ceiling.

John walked to the steel doors, shone his flashlight on the combination dials and began to manipulate them. Then he turned the lever-shaped handles and the doors swung open. "Paul," he said, stepping into the darkness, "kill that light switch for red back there, huh?" I did and John once again stepped into the darkness, reached out his right hand and waited until he assumed I was beside him in the darkness. "Now," John almost whispered and then turned on the light switch.

"God!" Was all I could say. Thinking about it later, I realized I had never questioned John on how there was light. Frankly, at that point, if John had snapped his fingers and said, "Let there be light," I would have fully expected that there would be. The answer to this and many other questions would come later.

CHAPTER THIRTY-ONE

He looked at me, smiled, and stepped down into the great room. "Just as I described it," he said, with what I could tell was justifiable pride.

John suggested that we bring the bikes down the ramp and he pointed to his left, to the far side of the three broad stone steps leading into the great room. He promised to give me a quick tour before I collapsed. I could just imagine how bad I looked like at this juncture; I definitely knew what I felt like.

He started his liberated Harley down the ramp, stopped it, went back, and closed the doors from the inside, sliding a bar in place across the double doors. "Place is stone, so it's fireproof; everything in it is as fireproof as possible. I've got a couple of emergency exits too; show 'em to you tomorrow."

John returned to the Harley and started it down the ramp, stopping again to hit another light switch mounted against the cave wall, metal wire molding running from it up toward the darkness of the ceiling. The ramp was wide enough for us to walk our bikes side by side. In front of us, at the base of the ramp, Rourke pointed out a truck.

"Ford, four-wheel drive pickup, converted it to run off pure ethyl alcohol. Got a distillery for it set up on the far side over there." He pointed well beyond the camouflage-painted pickup truck to the far end of the side cavern. Along the natural rock wall, separating it from the main cavern, were rows upon rows of shelves stacked floor to ceiling and several large ladders spaced along their length.

He had everything! His earlier descriptions to me did not do justice to what I was seeing now. I saw spare ammunition, reloading components when it would be necessary, food, whiskey, and whatever. John parked the bike on its stand and I did the same with mine. He walked the length of the side cavern, pointing to the shelves. "I've got a complete inventory that I run on an ascending/descending balance system, so I know what's running down, what might spoil, et cetera." Then, he started pinpointing, calling off the things on the shelves.

"Toilet paper, paper towels, bath soap, shampoo and conditioner, candles, light bulbs—sixties, hundreds—fluorescent tubes, light switches, screws, nails, bolts, nuts, washers."

He stopped to point to a low shelf—"McCulloch Pro Mac 610 chain saw—best there is; combines easy handling with near professional quality durability—spare parts, et cetera." Moving on, he said, "Here is the ammunition for my guns." He pointed at the .22 Long Rifle shells, then .38 Specials. Next was .357 Magnum, 9mm Parabellum, .44 Magnum and .45 ACP round. Next, the rifle cartridges; .223s, .308s. He had shotgun ammo; twelve-gauge in double 00 buckshot and rifled slugs, mostly the two and three-quarter inch rounds. "I stick to the shorter stuff," Rourke commented, "because it works in the three-inch Magnums, not vice-versa."

I only had a vague idea of what he was talking about. There was too much data and not enough references in my mind to comprehend anything other than he was well-stocked. There was row upon row of Mountain House foods in large containers and small packages; some were ordinary canned goods, other food supplies, stacks of white boot socks, underpants, and handkerchiefs. A large bin occupied some of the end of the shelving area. Inside it he showed me holsters, slings, and various other leather goods. Beyond this was a shelf filled with a dozen pair of black GI combat boots and beside these a half dozen pairs of rubber thongs.

"It'll take you a while," John said, "before you can really see all I've put up but you'll catch on to it. Check the inventory sheets." He took down one of four clipboards hanging on hooks at the far end of the shelving. "Now, look behind you. My pride and joy..." he said as he gestured to the far wall. A gleaming black Harley-Davidson Low Rider suspended a few inches off the floor— "to protect the tires."

He walked back to the end of the shelf row and hit another switch and the side cavern behind us went dark; hitting a second switch, the darkened smaller chamber ahead of them illuminated.

"Work room," John said and pointed along the walls and down a row of long tables to vises, reloading equipment, power saws, and a drill press. Arranged on shelves above these were oil filters, spark plugs, fan belts; tools hung on pegboard wall panels beyond these. Rourke set his CAR-15 on one of the tables and withdrew the Python, setting it beside the rifle. Next, he snatched both Detonics pistols from their double-shoulder rig and set them down as well and then the small A.G. Russell black chrome Sting 1A.

Holding up the Sting, John told me, "This was introduced in the 1970s and a fix for the other poorly designed boot knives. A friend of mine, A.G. Russell from Arkansas, came up with it. Boot knives, small blades sometimes called a Gambler's Dagger, were intended for personal defense. His great-grandfather taught him how to make knives when he was nine. He had wanted the Sting to be used as a backup knife for hunting as well as defense. It was a tough knife from the beginning. The original model was fitted with the wood handle. When the Sting 1A was released, it was one piece of steel having no added handle slabs. They are sometimes called 'skeleton' knives for that reason and the Russell knife was one of the first skeleton knives, being the first from a commercial source. A.G. went on to co-found the Knife Collectors Club and the Knifemarkers' Guild. Gotta clean all of these tomorrow," Rourke said.

I took the Browning High Power from my belt, set it down, and then laid down the Schmeisser. "I'll get the little Lawman and the Steyr later," John said. "Come on." He walked past the rows of tables, hit the light switch, and then turned a corner. Once again, we were in the main cavern but at the far end of the great room, I heard water splashing. In the cave was a waterfall; icy water careening over the edge at least forty feet below into a pool at its base.

Looking at the falls, I thought about a guy I had worked with in New York who took his family on a vacation trip to Tennessee a year or so back. One of the tourist attractions they visited was Ruby Falls, which is one of the deepest commercial caves in the world. He said you could take an elevator deep down into the cave. A tour guide talked about all the natural rock formations and how the creation of the falls was approximately 30 million years ago. Karl, my co-worker, was not at all comfortable down there; it was no place for someone feeling claustrophobic, but he didn't want to freak out in front of his kids. Well, near the end of the tour, they were all herded into a large cavern, almost like a theater without seating. Everyone gathered together, organ music started playing, and colored lights illuminated the walls and the ceiling. In front of them loomed this massive waterfall, thundering over the rocks above and pouring down into the inky darkness below them. He said it was like a religious experience; beautiful and totally awesome.

That is how I felt when I first entered the great room. How do I describe it? For the first time in as long as I could remember I felt... safe. I felt like I was home; a home I had never seen or even imagined. I trusted my life to John Rourke and he brought me through hell fire. Feelings? I hadn't been able to afford feelings lately. I had been in such a state of mental and emotional overwhelm, not to mention on more than one occasion, absolute physical and spiritual exhaustion. Was it really finally over? God I needed rest.

John stripped away his leather jacket, his Alessi shoulder rig, and the Ranger leather belt and set them on the arm of what looked like a leather-covered chair. "Vinyl," he identified. "Hate the stuff, but it's less susceptible to damage than leather and more easily repaired." He started into the room, then stopped, turned to me, and took off his sunglasses. "What would you like to see first? I bet the bathroom, hmm? How about a real shower?" My tired, aching body would have jumped for joy if it could have stood the effort.

Not waiting for an answer, he started toward the near side of the great room, walked up a row of three low stone steps, and pointed toward the opaque curtain of stone. "In there—help yourself. Grab yourself some clothes. I'll use it later."

Then he turned and walked across the great room toward the television set, the stereo, the books, and the guns. He stopped in front of the glass gun case and slid the glass panel aside. I had a handful of clean clothes and was eager for that shower, but first I had to ask, "What's that, John?"

"Come and see," he said, staring back at the cabinet. I stopped beside him, "That's an Interdynamics KG-9, 9mm assault pistol.

"Looks like a submachine gun," I said.

"Only a semi-automatic though," Rourke said then pointed to each succeeding item, identifying it in turn: a Smith and Wesson Model 29 six-inch, Metalifed and Mag-Na-Ported; Smith and Wesson Model 60 two-inch stainless Chiefs .38 Special; Colt Mk IV, Series '70 Government Model; Metalifed with a Detonics Competition Recoil system installed and Pachmayr Colt Medallion grips.

One little thing was a FIE .38 Special chrome Derringer. The little tubes that he pointed out to me on the shelf were .22 Long Rifle and .25 ACP barrel inserts made by someone named Harry Owens of Sport Specialties, which enabled the little gun to fire .38 Special, .22 rim fire, or .25 ACP. He had more of those insert barrels for the Detonics, his shotguns, et cetera. Rourke pointed back up to the cabinet. It held a Colt Official Police .38 Special five-inch—Metalifed with Pachmayr grips, reamed out to .357 to increase its versatility. There was a standard AR-15, no scope, a Mossberg 500ATP6P Parkerized riot shotgun, and an original Armalite AR-7 .22 Long Rifle. You could take it apart and stow the action in the butt stock. He told me it would float.

"How much... I mean it's rude, John, I know that, but how..."

"Every cent I could scrape together for the last six years, after the cost of the property itself. It wasn't cheap, but I gambled it would be necessary one day. I'm sorry I won, but it paid off I guess." He loosed the case and walked toward the sofa in the center of the great room and then leaned down to a small box on the table and looked inside. "Empty," he muttered and crossed the room. He glanced over his shoulder; I was following him. Rourke smiled, saying, "You're more curious than eager for that shower, aren't you?"

"How did you get all of this up here?"

"With the truck," he answered, as he went to the refrigerator, opened it, and took out an ice tray. He took a large glass beer mug from an overhead cabinet and filled it half with ice. He replaced the unused ice cubes, muttering, "Help yourself to anything you want," then turned on a small black switch next to the sink. There was a rumble, a mechanical hum, then he turned on the cold water faucet, the spigot sputtering a moment. "Air gets in the system," Rourke remarked, then water spattered out; Rourke walked away, leaving the water running.

He went to another cabinet, this time below the counter level, and extracted a half-gallon bottle of Seagram's Seven, twisted off the cap, breaking the stamp, and poured a good three inches in the beer mug over the ice. He then closed the bottle and replaced it under the counter. He returned to the sink and added two inches of water to the glass, shut off the water, and then turned off the pump switch. "You've always got to remember to turn on the switches for the water; that is the only thing different from ordinary plumbing. I use several electrically and manually operated pumps, so if one breaks down, it won't kill all my water at once."

Rourke started out of the kitchen and back down the steps into the great room. I was right behind him. "John, this can't be real, I mean—"

"It is, Paul," he said, turning. "It is." He suggested that I get cleaned up and promised to fix us something to eat."

"How about steak and eggs?" I asked laughing.

Rourke didn't laugh. "Well, I'll have to flash thaw it, but I guess so. Powdered eggs all right?"

He nursed his drink while I showered.

CHAPTER THIRTY-TWO

We had taken "cowboy showers" in the field; John was a stickler on hygiene. He told me often that if we don't take care of our bodies they can't take care of us. There was less chance of infection if we stayed as clean as possible. After I got out of the hospital in East Texas, I had been able to take a real shower, but there were about twenty other men doing the same thing.

This was the first time in I couldn't remember when that I had the bathroom and shower all to myself. I sat on the toilet without watching over my shoulder for some threat and I got to use real toilet paper, an uncommon treat. The shower was scalding and it felt incredible. I lathered and rinsed and lathered and rinsed again. I felt clean; the days of filth and sweat drained away. I washed my hair and even used some conditioner. I didn't recognize my own scent.

I dried off and walked to the sink for a shave. I stepped back from the mirror; I didn't recognize myself. I stared at the man looking back from the glass; I didn't know him. His face was tanned and had none of the "baby fat" I remembered.

The arms belied strength; the shoulders seemed broader, possibly because the waist was a lot smaller. I had used all the holes in my belt and had used John's knife to make two more. I thought I was just losing weight, but that wasn't it at all... I had moved it and transformed it. After all, now I was more physically active—riding a motorcycle when I was only used to riding a desk.

The transformation surprised me but honestly it pleased me also. There was a man staring back at me. Not a kid, not a nerd; a genuine honest to gosh man with a stronger chin line and a straighter, leaner, stronger body. I looked at my hands. I had not seen them clean and washed in a long time. There were calluses where none had ever been. I flexed them and watched the muscles and ligaments moving. I was noticing parts of me I had never seen before. I hadn't felt the change. I hadn't dieted. I hadn't gone to the gym. But there a new man stood. I remember talking to one of my friends who had entered the military; when he came back from Basic Training, he too was transformed.

"It works like this," he had explained. "If you're overweight when you get there, you'll lose weight. If you're underweight, you'll gain. Either way, you get stronger." I had finished my first episode of basic training, and it had worked.

CHAPTER THIRTY-THREE

John had gotten the steaks and set the microwave oven, returning to the sofa by the time I returned. He was reading, not a book but a catalogue of the books he had on the shelves along one wall of the great room, refreshing himself on the contents of his library and determining now that it was his only library, if any gaps existed that critically needed filling.

When I came back into the room, he put down the loose-leaf binder. He went to the bookshelves, rolled the ladder along their length and climbed up, selecting a book about projected climatologically changes as the result of heat and temperature inversion. The red sunsets still worried him.

"All those books, John. What are these?" I stopped and pointed to a lower shelf.

"Just books I've written on weapons, survivalism, things like that. I've tried to have something of everything," he said, sipping his drink and studying the cover of the book, as if by holding it, an answer to the bizarre climate would somehow come to him osmotically. "I always viewed a library as the most essential thing for survival beyond food, water, shelter, and weapons. What good would it do if we survived, Paul, if all the wisdom of the world were lost to us? I may be misquoting, but I believe it was Einstein who said that regardless of what World War III was fought with—and I'm just paraphrasing—World War IV would be fought with rocks and clubs. Simply, it means that civilization—regardless of the physical reality of man—would end. It won't here." Rourke gestured broadly toward his books.

"Children's books too?" I looked at the lowest shelf.

"For Annie and Michael, perhaps their children someday. Can't teach them to read with these." Rourke gestured at the higher shelves. "Most of those children's books were illustrated or written and illustrated by Sarah anyway—a double purpose."

"Do you really think it'll last that long?"

"The world or the aftermath of the War?" Rourke asked, turning away, not expecting an answer. He dropped the book on the coffee table, looked over his shoulder as he downed his drink. "If the timer hits on the microwave, just push the off button. I'm taking a shower. Oh, and feel free to make yourself a drink."

While John showered I took a more thorough look around, trying to take in some of the things I had previously missed. "Will wonders never cease?" crossed my mind over and over again. When he came back, he stopped and smiled after he saw the look of bewilderment on my face. "You're impressed?"

"A greenhouse?" I said, staring at a small house of sheet plastic, humidity dripping from the windows and bright purple lights glowing from within.

"I wish I could use sunlight but if I installed any sort of skylight, it would be visible from the air; that could blow the whole place. So, as long as the grow lights hold out, we've got fresh vegetables, occasionally."

I punched the off button on the microwave oven I'd forgotten about, not noticing the incessant buzz. "You got everything here!" I exclaimed.

"Not quite," Rourke said then walked back in the kitchen. We ate; Rourke in relative silence. I could tell he wasn't in a talkative mood, so I finished the meal and went to bed—my own bed with a mattress, clean sheets, and a pillow. I felt safe. I was in heaven and could hear the angels singing softly as my head hit the pillow. Then I experienced blissful, deep, and dark sleep.

CHAPTER THIRTY-FOUR

"Hello, Paul, were you trying for an endurance record?" he said. I had slept fourteen hours. It was the first time I wasn't worried that somebody was going to shoot me in the middle of the night or something. Rourke was sitting at the kitchen counter, staring into the empty great room and sipping his own strong black coffee. He had arisen early, Rourke time of six A.M. He told me he had cleaned the guns, including my High Power and MP-40 and then performed the necessary maintenance on the liberated Harley Low Rider, checking his own machine. And had gotten out the Lowe Alpine Systems Loco pack, the kind used by search and rescue teams, but had put off loading it, being hungry. He poured another cup of coffee, working with pencil and paper.

He would leave soon to scout the area for Soviet and brigand activity and to pick up the trail of Sarah and the children. He had noted several items on his checklist: both of the Detonics pistols, the small Musette bag with spare magazines and ammo, the Bushnell 8x30 armored binoculars, and the big, handmade Chris Miller Bowie knife.

"Have some coffee," John said as I went up the three stone steps into the kitchen. "There's orange juice in the refrigerator. Just look around and fix yourself some breakfast."

"John?" I began, pouring myself a steaming mug of coffee. "My parents—I want to go down to St. Petersburg, see if there still is a St. Petersburg and see if they're alive."

"I know," he said then smiled at me. "I'll miss you, Paul. I'll always count you my best friend..."

"Take whatever you need to get there and stay alive. I've got plenty and I can get more."

"No, I didn't—I mean; if they're dead, would you..."

"My home—mi casa es su casa, amigo. Yeah, I'd like it if things work out that way. And for your sake, I hope they don't, but I'd like it if you came back. I could use your help finding Sarah and the children; the kids could use an uncle."

"But, you can't leave for a while; remember I'm a doctor? You need about a week of rest before those wounds will be healed enough for you to travel hard alone."

He told me that when he returned, he'd teach me some things before I left; a couple of tricks that might just help me stay alive. He wanted to give me a good knife, some maps, and a good compass. And show me how to use it and how to take care of my bike; some which I already knew. But most importantly, he'd show me how to clean and care for my guns and put a good edge on my knife. These things would be imperative to know if I was going to stay alive.

CHAPTER THIRTY-FIVE

"John, do you think you're going to find them—Sarah and the children, I mean?" I asked, sipping coffee from the mug.

"Yeah, I've thought about it. And yeah, I'll find them, no matter what. You..." Rourke paused as he stood up, pouring himself another cup of coffee. He leaned against the counter, staring past me toward the great room. "You know, we never seem to have much time just to talk, you and I."

"I think Natalia always wondered about me, what makes me tick. I decided years ago, back in Latin America, that time I had to stay alive on my own after the CIA team I was with got ambushed and I was wounded. The thing that makes one person stay alive no matter what and another person buy it—there's some luck to it, sure. The toughest man or woman on earth can be at ground zero of a nuclear blast and he's still going to die. But under general conditions, what makes one person survive and another lose is—well, there're a lot of names for it."

"Some people call it meanness; some call it tenaciousness—whatever. But it's will—you will yourself not to die, not to give up. Nobody out there's going to kill me," he said, gesturing toward the steel doors leading into the entrance hall and the outside world beyond. "Nobody out there's going to kill me or stop me—unless I let them do it. Sure, somebody could be up in the rocks and blow the back of my head open with a sniper rifle and you can't control that—but in a situation, a conflict," Rourke struggled for the right words—"it's not that I'm any better or tougher or smarter. I just won't quit. You know what I mean, Paul? It's hard to explain, really."

"I know—I've seen that in you," I said. "Yeah, you want to teach me that?"

"I couldn't if I wanted to—and I don't need to. You just need to sharpen a few more of the skills that'll let you stay alive. You've got enough will. I don't worry about you out there any more than I worry about myself. You're a good man. I haven't said that to very many people," Rourke concluded, staring back at his list while sipping his coffee. As I made my breakfast, I was vaguely aware of the sounds of the water from the falls and the water crashing down into the pool.

He wrote something on the list, the one item he said made his skin crawl, because of what it represented— "Geiger counter." He swallowed his coffee and almost burned his mouth.

I looked at Rourke and thought about his words. I couldn't imagine the things he'd seen, that made him into the man that was now sitting in front of me. Some would call him mean, I called him purposeful. Some would call him hard; I knew he had become hard in order to survive. But underneath that steel veneer was a man, a husband, a father and my friend. Complex, but without being complicated; he was purposeful, with a damnable ability to find his purpose in any situation we encountered. He acted when others hesitated. He had cultivated this persona; it was the only way he believed he had a chance to survive that which most would think was unsurvivable.

CHAPTER THIRTY-SIX

Rourke told me he'd be back within four days or less, but experience had taught him to prepare for three times that period. The pack was strapped to the back of the Harley with food, medical supplies, clothing—all the necessities. Two straps crossed his chest. On his left side hung the Musette bag with some of his spare ammo and a few packages of dehydrated fruit that he'd made himself.

On his right hung binoculars; beneath them, his Colt Government MK IV series '70 .45. The twin Detonics stainless pistols hung in the double Alessi rig under his arms. The gun belt around his waist carried spare Colt magazines for the Government, and these also doubled with the Detonics pistols. From the left side of his belt hung a bayonet for the M-16. It fit the CAR-15 slung across Rourke's back, muzzle down and muzzle cap off, a thirty-round magazine inserted. He squinted against the sun despite the aviator sunglasses he wore, mounted the Harley again and headed onto the road, leaning back and letting the machine out, waving as though he were going out for a Sunday afternoon jaunt.

CHAPTER THIRTY-SEVEN

I spent the time he was gone resting, cleaning, preparing my equipment, and studying. It was the first "downtime," as John called it, I had known. His library covered every subject I looked for. I read books on guns, ammo, and knives. I was able to fill in some of the blanks that his education had left me with. John was incredibly intense; the speed at which things had been coming at me was just too fast-paced. I needed more time to assimilate facts, to take raw knowledge and understand it.

I read and took notes, correlating the bits and pieces of information he had thrown at me with such vigor and force. Usually, these bits and pieces were flung as other people were shooting lead or throwing high explosives at us. I began to get a better understanding and was better able to identify the relevance of what, for me at least, had been disjointed pieces of information. Each piece was terribly important, but I didn't operate in the framework of knowledge that John had spent years constructing.

It all started making sense to me, how bits of data could be linked, like words linked to form sentences and paragraphs. Words could tell entire stories. Facts, once related and connected, ceased to be meaningless garbled noise. Now, I was really learning. It felt good; maybe my thoughts would catch up to the body I had built. At least that was my thought that day; in reality, my education would be a life-long experience.

And for the first time in years... I read the Torah. I found a copy one day in John's library. I guess he wanted to save it for whatever future might still be possible; that fit with the other things he had saved and stockpiled.

I devoured it, the stories of my people and our God. I was like a dried out husk, the moisture slowly seeping back into my pores. I had not realized how empty I was before this adventure started.

During the day I toured the Retreat, getting familiar with what John had stockpiled and trying to understand the significance of each item. At night I rested or at least tried to rest but my dreams were chaotic, confused. Ruth came to me often; most of the time we didn't talk. I tried explaining what had happened, but she rarely commented; she would just sit there with a forlorn expression on her face.

I came to realize the dreams were just that, dreams. I remembered that song from Jiminy Cricket and the line that said, "A dream is a wish your heart makes." My heart, at this time, did not have a wish. While my conscious mind was being filled with new data, my heart was empty except for the longing and misery associated with my lost world, my lost parents and the loss of the girl I loved.

CHAPTER THIRTY-EIGHT

Now that I had figured out how John cataloged his storehouse of knowledge, I went searching for a three-inch, loose leaf binder with "Retreat Operations Manual" on the cover. The shock of being in the Retreat was over, but I still had a question from that first entry into it. How the hell had the lights come on? I didn't question it at the time. Rourke flipped a switch, therefore the lights were supposed to come on; simple as that.

But there was no electrical grid. How the hell did we have hot water for showers? How did all the electrical appliances work? What was the power source in a world that had been thrown back over a hundred years in technological development? The answers were all here. One the first page of the manual were notes Rourke had written to himself, "Keep It Simple Stupid," "Old Knowledge Trumps Technology Anytime," "Magic is simply science unexplained," and "Redundancy is the friend of success."

Rourke had truly Planned Ahead. Water for example was not only a primary consideration for surviving; it was Rourke's primary power source. The stream and waterfall I had grown so used to were where it all started. He had built water powered generators, same principle as Hoover Damn, but on a small scale. Those generators created electricity and provided power to a bank of storage batteries that stood ready to provide power. Ergo, the lights had worked. Once the batteries were at full charge, the electricity went directly to whatever appliance was turned on.

All of these were connected to something he called "multipliers." As best as I could understand it, the multipliers used electric current to create even more electricity. While I didn't really understand the mechanics of it all, it was simple and effective. While he knew a closed circuit "perpetual motion" generator was an impossibility, he had come awfully close to it with this system.

And he didn't power everything. Why use power when weights and counter-weights functioned just as well, using nothing more than levers and gravity. When all else failed, for emergencies, he had generators that operated off of both gasoline and pure grain alcohol, which he could brew in his own still. I won't bore you with the details, let me just say it was very simple once you understood Rourke's plan—it worked.

Suddenly I stopped reading, aware of something for the first time. I had found a teacher, someone that could and would educate me. John had to teach himself all of this information. Michael and Annie were too young to appreciate it and Sarah, by John's presentation, could care less. What is worse than a student without a teacher? A teacher without a student. A student can reject knowledge and be satisfied, but a teacher HAS to teach and see a student learn and cognite or their soul will shrivel. When the student is craving knowledge and questioning, it is like iron sharpening iron. The teacher is as involved as the student, both brains expanded—the student gets better and the teacher has to stretch. That is where a degree of fulfillment comes from—teaching. Rourke had taught himself much but with little interaction with others. When he had been a student, he had been part of that "dance."

That had been missing during the creation and development of the Retreat. Sure, John Rourke was a leader and an "action man," he was also a "teacher." And a teacher has to have a student or he is incomplete. He would one day teach Michael and Annie but all the while he was preparing the Retreat, he sincerely never wanted to have to use it. I wondered, *Will they understand what he did and how much he spent of himself to do this? Probably not, after all, he's just Dad.* Suddenly, I couldn't see clearly. When I removed my wire frame glasses, I realized tears were running down my face.

Preparing all these years, all the effort in the hope it would never be used... I saw for the first time that I was actually reciprocating with John. I wasn't just a drain on his time and energy; he needed me as much as I needed him. Just in a different way; *how lonely he must have been at times*, I thought. I wondered if he had ever thought these thoughts, then I realized, *Of course at some level, he must have. After all, he's John Rourke.*

I wondered if he and I would ever discuss my realizations, *Probably not, after all he's John Rourke.*

CHAPTER THIRTY-NINE

John got back earlier than I expected, and he had news. His news was difficult to believe and even more difficult to comprehend. We were not alone; and although hurt badly, America still existed. He had met up with American forces and there was an American Intelligence team that had been inserted in the area. His hair was still wet from the shower; he sat on the couch, a glass of Seagram's Seven in his right hand and a cigar burning in the ashtray beside him.

"Paul! What do you think, have you ever heard of the Eden Project, something to do with Cape Canaveral; what does it suggest?" he asked me.

I thought for several moments then looked up and said, "Well, the Eden reference seems to mean some sort of beginning—maybe beginning again."

"Yeah," Rourke agreed.

"So, maybe it's some sort of manned flight that would have been too risky, unless there wasn't anything to lose. A lot of people thought the world would just get flattened after a full nuclear exchange, maybe it was some sort of space colonization effort or something."

"Or maybe just the opposite—a doomsday device. You've got to remember one thing, Paul, intelligence-operations names rarely have anything to do with the actual operation—just the opposite—so maybe a new beginning simply means a surprise ending."

"You mean some kind of super bomb orbiting the earth and timed to blow up soon?"

"Maybe not soon," Rourke said soberly. "Maybe not for five years, or ten years, or maybe the next five minutes. And maybe it's nothing we've thought of. I'll tell you what Reed, that's the guy in charge of the American forces around here, wants me to do," Rourke said, recounting his conversation with the Army captain and their scheduled meeting the next day. Rourke looked at his watch. It was already the next day—15 minutes into it. We talked for a while longer and then he went to bed before me.

CHAPTER FORTY

With this new information gleaned by John's meeting with the captain, he had begun to construct his next plan for finding Sarah and the kids. He planned to leave in a few days. My body was repaired and I was ready to begin my own search.

John agreed I was ready, so for the next two days he trained me to be alone and how to protect myself and protect my gear. I'd be going into humid air so he showed me how to clean and protect my guns from rusting, and where carbon and unburnt powder normally clings to a gun and the best way to get it out. It took me three tries before he finally passed my cleaning efforts.

He oversaw as I packed a cleaning kit and knife sharpeners. I would have a limited amount of food, water, ammo and gasoline. I would constantly be on the lookout for ways to resupply what I was able to take with me.

I learned how to aim, how to shoot, how to quickly reload. I learned how to navigate, read maps... build fires without matches. I learned how to rig a shelter, how to use a knife... how to dig a slit trench—you have to go to the bathroom some time. It was like trying to put a gallon of coffee in an eight ounce cup. A lot spilled over; I just couldn't soak it all in, in such a short time.

Then he showed me how to hold a knife when I sharpened it. How to "get the right angle" against the sharpening rocks, which he said were Arkansas soft and hard whetstones. He showed me how much oil to use, and how to keep it from clogging the pores in the whet rocks, and how to scrape the same number of times on both sides of the blade. "You sharpen a knife the same way you sharpen a man," he said. "First you rub it up against something that is harder than it, or he is. You take the same number of strokes on both sides of the blade; that keeps the edge balanced," he continued. "But the most important aspect is you have to find the right angle." I wondered if he was still talking about steel in his hand, or the steel within a man.

My Reflections:

Looking back, I remember thinking about John, Michael and Annie, and tears filling my eyes. If he found them, he'd have so much to teach the kids about survival. There's no way they would really understand what their father was about to teach them. At a young age, kids accept the "data" just because... after all, he's Dad and dads know everything. As they get older, they don't always "accept" that guidance as easily. Part of that is usually because kids have no idea what a father has gone through to gain that knowledge. It is those unknown nuances' that add depth and understanding to the information. What does it cost a father in time, mistakes and missteps? All fathers try to keep their kids from making the mistakes they had made.

My tears had come from realizing I didn't know my own Dad very well. I knew he had always been there, but I had no idea of the journey he had been on. The times he failed, his disappointments, the times he was embarrassed, the things he had endured to launch me on my own path. I wondered if Michael and Annie would ever really get to know their father. I also wondered if my own parents were still alive; would I ever see them again? Would I have time to "learn" them?

I pondered John's news; we weren't alone and not all of the rest of the world had reverted to savagery. There was hope and help outside the Retreat—John had found it. What did that mean to our overall situation? I didn't know but for the first time in a long time I thought, *Maybe, just maybe, we can get out of this alive and rebuild.*

As John had to try and find his family, I knew I must try also. Would either of us be successful? Probably not. Most likely we would die in a hail of bullets or some other calamity—but, we had to try.

I often thought about what John had said about sharpening a knife. "You sharpen a knife the same way you sharpen a man," he said. "First you rub it up against something that is harder than it, or he is." Since the Night of the War, I had rubbed against a lot of things harder than me. And like a knife, these things were sharpening me, making me stronger—they were making me a man.

PART IV

MEETING THE DOOMSAYER

CHAPTER FORTY-ONE

John and I left the same day. I set out for Florida in a quest for my parents to see if somehow they had survived the holocaust of the Night of the War—World War III. John set out for on his search for Sarah and the kids. He was headed toward one of the strategic fuel reserve sites the new President of the United States II, Samuel Chambers, had pinpointed for him. I knew where the ones on my route MIGHT still be found, if I made it that far.

*****

"Shit," I muttered, my collar up against the wind, asking half under my breath, "Why is it cold in St. Petersburg?" I looked around me, down at the Harley and at the Schmeisser slung under my right arm, deciding nothing in view could or would answer me. Pushing my wire-framed glasses up from the bridge of my nose, I levered out the Harley's stand, dismounted, and moved into the trees to get further off the road below and avoid the wind. I dropped to the ground; squatting there, wishing I had brought some cigarettes.

I could still see the road through the trees and watched to make certain none of the troops moving along below made any sudden moves toward the side of the road where I was hiding. I could tell by their uniforms they were Cuban. Of course, since I didn't speak Spanish, that didn't do me much good.

I wondered for an instant what John was doing. Had he found Sarah and the children yet? If he hadn't, how long would he keep on looking? I studied the road, drawing casually in the dirt between my legs with the point of the Gerber Mark II knife John had given me for the journey. Mentally, I began to tick off the situation's pertinent details, to help myself form a plan.

CHAPTER FORTY-TWO

I had been in the St. Petersburg area for nearly three days. The city itself was partially destroyed; there were internment concentration camps all over. I studied the faces inside, behind the wire fences. I'd convinced myself most of the people inside were old and seemed to be Jewish. I knew it was just a feeling. Maybe they weren't Jewish; perhaps it was the armed guards and the barbed wire that made me think of the films of the camps during World War II. I decided some of them were Jewish at least.

It was now dark. I left the bike and slipped quietly through the streets past the Communist Cuban patrols. The house my parents had lived in was gone. Next to it was a house with a roof and three standing walls; there had been a fire and obvious looting. My folks were not there.

I checked throughout the neighborhood, trying to remember which houses belonged to their friends I had met the few times I had visited them there. I wasn't certain of any of it, but none of the houses in the neighborhood looked to be inhabited or habitable anymore.

I eventually came to one large camp, larger than many of the others combined. I told myself there would be someone inside the camp who knew my parents, and perhaps knew what had happened to them. If they were dead, I wanted to know for certain. I knew that concentration camps were made to keep people in, not out. I smiled with the thought that after I penetrated the main camp and learned what I could, I could free some of the prisoners.

"God!" The thing crawling quickly around the base of the palm tree behind which I was hidden, looked to be the largest roach I'd ever seen in my life. "Eyuck!" I'd read an article once about roaches, and it didn't surprise me that they survived the Night of the War. Some scientists theorized that if all other life on the planet were to be killed, roaches and rats might still thrive. I decided this was a wood roach or American cockroach. Smiling, pushing my glasses up off the bridge of my nose, I saluted the creature, muttering, "My fellow American..."

I stared beyond the palm to where my real "fellow Americans" were located. Some of the faces I observed were Hispanic-looking, probably anti-Communist Cubans; some of the faces looked Central European in origin. Some, I thought, were Jews like me. I found the barbed wire particularly nauseating, people living behind it. I mentally saw again the pictures I had seen of the ghettos in Poland and other places during the Second World War.

It all brought back images of the death camps at Auschwitz, Dora/Mittelbau and its sub-camp, Buchenwald. These were images I never thought I would see, except in history books, certainly not in person and certainly not in America.

CHAPTER FORTY-THREE

I traced my route back to the motorcycle and brought it up closer to the main camp. I moved slowly on it through the woods; no light and as little noise as I could get away with. Thirty minutes later, I left the motorcycle about a mile away in a wooded area. I would go the rest of the way on foot. After scouting the perimeter of the camp, I selected the spot least visible between the guard towers and decided on it as my point of entry.

I had brought the big Gerber knife, the Browning High Power, the Schmeisser and spare loaded magazines for each of the guns. I studied the camp, smiling to myself. The Schmeisser, a weapon originally developed for the Nazi war machine, was now going to help me break into a concentration camp and perhaps break out some of the inmates.

When I first entered St. Petersburg, I found a deserted farm implements store, the windows smashed. I took a pair of long-handled wire cutters; and yes, I checked for radiation with the Geiger counter on my Harley.

I remembered in Albuquerque, that first night we had teamed up, when John and I had broken into the back room of the geological supply store and stolen the flashlights. John had said then that it was no longer stealing; it was foraging. I smiled at the thought; I had foraged the wire cutters.

It looked to me like a good hundred yards from the farthest edge of the tree line to the outer fence. Beyond the first wire fence, a barren patch extended perhaps twenty-five yards. I studied the ground through the armored binoculars—identical to the ones John used. There were no signs of recent digging or depressions in the sparsely grassed ground. I hoped it was not mined.

At the end of the twenty-five yards of open ground was another fence, ten feet high, and this one might be electrified. I wasn't certain, but I noticed that none of the guards walked even close to it—that made me wonder. Beyond that was another ten feet or so of open ground then a six-foot high barbed wire fence. People leaned against this fence, staring out; what they stared at I didn't know. I wondered if they knew.

I spent my time in the dark observing the pattern of the guards. I checked the Timex on my left wrist and decided to go exactly on the hour, and that was in five more minutes. Running in a low crouch, I started out of the palms and toward the first of the ten foot wire fences, the Schmeisser slung from my right shoulder and the wire cutters in my left hand. I was a little winded by the time I crossed the distance to the first fence. As I reached it, I dropped into a deeper crouch, glancing quickly from side to side with the wire cutters already moving in my hands.

Starting at the bottom of the fence, I clipped a single cut, approximately four feet high. Because of the heaviness of the wire, another cut was needed. Slipping through the darkness, I cut horizontally across the top of the first cut, pulling the barbed wire outward and the "gate" in the wire closed behind me. I glanced toward the guard towers then hit the dirt, flattening the Schmeisser out in my right hand. A searchlight beam crossed over the ground less than a foot away from me.

The searchlight moved on and so did I, running across the grassy area, zigzagging just in case there was a minefield, hoping by some miracle I'd miss them all by not running in a straight line. I made the opposite fence line, breathless again. I started to reach my hand toward it then stopped, my hand recoiling. There was a rat on the ground less than a foot from me, the body half-burned. "Electrified," I cursed.

I glanced from side to side, quickly trying to determine whether to go back or whether there was some other way to cross the fence. "Damnit!" I muttered, then snatched the big Gerber knife and started digging in the mixed dirt and sand. I couldn't go through the fence and couldn't go over it, so I'd go under it.

I glanced up, flattening myself on the ground, sucking in my breath, almost touching the fence. The searchlight moved down the center of the open space between the fences, missing me by inches. As soon as it passed, keeping myself as low to the ground as possible, I started to dig again.

For once, I was grateful I wasn't as big or as broad shouldered as Rourke. I scooped dirt with my hands, widening the hole under the fence. The searchlight was making another pass and I went flat again, as close to the fence as possible. This time, I noticed the searchlight scanned more frequently and more rapidly, the ground between this fence and the interior fence.

That area, at least, was not electrified. Within the hour, all the prisoners in the compound had been herded inside the tents under which they were sheltered, and the compound grounds were empty of life. But earlier, I had seen hands and faces touching that fence. The small trench under the fence seemed wide enough now. Slipping into position, just missing another pass of the searchlight, I started through on my back. My shirt pulled out of my pants and I felt the dirt against the skin at the small of my back.

I stopped; the front of my shirt was stuck on a barb in the lowest strand of wire. Perhaps there was no power in the lowest strand, I thought and perhaps the material in the shirt just hadn't made the right contact. I didn't know and sucked my stomach in lest skin touched the barb. I looked from side to side, past the fence and back toward my feet, seeing the searchlight starting again. If I didn't do something, it would pass over my feet and reveal my presence.

I had a sick feeling; I had to gamble. I touched gingerly with my shirt-sleeved elbow at the wire. Nothing happened. I reached out with both hands, freeing my shirt front from the barb and then pushed through under the wire, the searchlight sweeping over the ground as my feet moved into the shadow. I was through!

I got to my feet, still in a crouch, and stared back at the wire a moment, reaching into the pockets of my leather jacket. There was nothing I could use, but I had to know. Taking the wire cutters, I reached under the fence's lowest strand and using the cutters like a slave hand in a laboratory, I picked up the dead rat and slid it under the fence toward me. I looked at the charred creature; I hated these things.

I lifted the rat with the tips of the cutters and tossed the already dead body against the wire second from the bottom of the fence, quickly drawing my right arm back toward my face.

The rodent clung to the wire a moment, smoking and electrical sparks flying. My stomach churned; I felt like throwing up, but instead I watched the searchlight as it swept toward me. I darted across the few feet of ground to the low fence, hiding beside it, gambling it wasn't electrified as I touched the cutters to the lowest strand and then the one above it. "Thank God," I whispered, letting out a long sigh. The search light passed inches from where I crouched as I began to cut the wire using the same pattern I used before. I cut up about four feet then three feet across the base of the fence, making a flap I could fold back and pull back into place.

Looking over my shoulder, the wire cutters in my left hand now, I folded back the fence section and started through into the compound. I folded the fence section back and in a crouch with the pistol grip of the Schmeisser in my right fist, the muzzle moving from side to side, I surveyed the compound.

I could see only one guard slowly moving around the grounds, fifty yards from where I was. Still holding the wire cutters, I started toward the nearest tent in a low, dead run. I pushed my way inside the tent and stopped; the smell nauseated me. There was a buzzing sound in the air as flies swarmed throughout the tent. I looked in the faces of the people under the glow of the single yellow light hanging from a drop cord in the center of the tent, the flies and moths buzzing close to it. It was disgusting to look at and the smell was even worse.

CHAPTER FORTY-FOUR

The faces were young and old, but all of them weary. Some of them were sleeping, flies crawling across them. There was a child, moaning beside a sleeping woman. I stepped closer to them and kicked away the mouse nibbling at the child's leg. I stood there a moment, tears welling up in my eyes and my glasses steaming a little. In that instant, I was thankful for the guns I carried and for the things I'd learned that had kept me from a similar fate. I was grateful to Rourke for teaching me how to survive after the Night of the War.

The phrase, "My fellow Americans" came to mind and how I'd thought of it earlier, as the roach climbed around the palm tree beyond the fences. I stood there crying, my right fist wrapped tightly on the Schmeisser.

CHAPTER FORTY-FIVE

I moved to the next tent and spoke with an older man; he was awake, swatting flies away from a festering wound on his left leg. Lights were kept on in the tents to make certain no one stood up during the night; and to make visual inspection of the tents easier when the guards looked in. There were no sanitary facilities or facilities for child care; and, some of the guards, the old man had confessed, enjoyed beating people. Some of the other guards seemed like decent men, the old man had told me, but they did nothing when the other guards began their beatings.

The old man had never heard of retired Air Force Colonel David Rubenstein or his wife. I went outside and threw up. When I got to the fifth tent, I forced my way inside, keeping low to avoid profiling myself in the yellow light. The stench in this tent was either not so bad or I had become accustomed to it; I don't know which.

There were more children here; faces drawn, eyes sunken, and bellies swollen. The old man, I didn't get his name, had said most of the older people gave the bulk of their food to the children and the recent mothers. The food allotment for each adult was a cup of cereal per day, as much bad water as you wanted to drink, and twice a week—fish or meat.

They said the cereal had weevils in it, while the fish and meat usually smelled rancid. Many around the camp had dysentery. I passed through the tent, looking for my parents or a familiar face, not sure if I'd recognize any of my parents' friends. There was a woman at the far end of the tent, holding a child in her arms, the child's breathing labored. She was awake and as I passed her, she whispered, "Who are you?"

"My name is Paul Rubenstein," I told her, glancing around the tent.

"Why are you here?"

"I'm looking for my parents. Do you know them? My father has a full head of white hair; his first name is David. My mother's first name is Rebecca, Rebecca Rubenstein. My father was a Colonel in the Air Force before he retired."

"He wouldn't be here then," the woman said. My throat had a catch in it, not sure what she meant and afraid to ask. "He just wouldn't be here. I was supposed to be someplace else too," she said, brushing a fly away from her child's lips, "but I was pregnant. They didn't want me along, so they left me. I lost the baby," she said, her voice even.

"I don't know what they did with my baby afterward. They never told me about him; he was a boy. My husband Ralph would have been proud of the boy—handsome. Ralph, he's in the Air Force too, that's why they took him. Some kind of special camp near Miami for military people and their families. I hope they don't hurt Ralph. I would have named my baby Ralph Jr., after my husband. He was a beautiful boy. I don't know what they did with him. I would have named him Ralph, you know."

All I could think to say was, "I'm sorry." Outside the tent, I crouched and cried quietly, "Goddamn them." It was starting to rain, and in the distance below the dark rain clouds, I could see a tiny knife edge of sunlight, reddish tinged. The camp would soon be awake; I had to get out, or I'd be caught.

I decided to go to Miami. I would find my parents at whatever hellhole camp they were in, if they were still alive. But first, I was going to do something here; I just didn't know what yet. There was the Army Intelligence contact; maybe he could help. I pulled myself back against the tent; I had heard the rumble of an engine. I saw off to my right a U.S. military jeep coming with three Cubans riding in it. The rain was coming down in sheets now and the wind was picking up. I pushed my glasses back from the bridge of my nose and pulled back the bolt on the Schmeisser, giving it a solid pat.

There I stood, Paul Rubenstein, about to enter a battle. Not to back up John Rourke—but one I was going to start myself. One part of my brain recognized the ludicrousness of the situation. The rest of my brain, powered by adrenalin and rage, forced that civilized part back into the darkness. I didn't have time to "think" like a civilized man. I was at war and about to engage the enemy. The scary thing to the civilized part of my mind was... I WANTED IT. I wanted to kill these bastards. I wanted to blow them to Hell.

Right now, this instant, they served as a focal point for all of my rage and fear. They were the personification of the evil that had destroyed my world, and I wanted their blood. I stood up, almost directly in front of the jeep, and at the top of my lungs shouted, "Eat lead you bastards!" and squeezed the trigger of the Schmeisser.

"Trigger control," I shouted, reiterating Rourke's constant warning, working the trigger out and in, keeping to three-round bursts from the thirty-round magazine. I hit the driver and then the man beside him; the third man in the back raised a pistol to fire. I pumped the Schmeisser's trigger again, emptying three rounds into the man's chest. He fell back, rolling down into the mud.

I ran beside the jeep, the vehicle going off at a crazy angle into one of the tents and jumped for it. With my left foot on the running board, I dropped the Schmeisser on the floorboard and shoved the dead driver out of the way. Sliding in, I kicked the dead man's feet away from the pedals.

Stopping the jeep, I rolled the body of the passenger and then the driver out the right side of the jeep and shifted into reverse. I grabbed the Schmeisser and put in a fresh magazine. People streamed from their tents as I skidded the jeep around, slamming on the brakes as I fumbled the transmission to first. I saw guards running toward them from the far end of the camp. With my jaw set and my lips curled back from my teeth, I stomped on the gas pedal, driving forward. The puddles sloshed up as I raced through the mud. Some of the prisoners threw themselves at the advancing Cuban guards.

"No!" I shouted as the guards machine-gunned the women and old people. I rested the blue-black submachine gun along the dashboard and started firing again. There were dozens of guards, all of them armed with assault rifles or pistols and streaming from metal huts. They were half-dressed, shouting, and firing at them. I kept shooting. On my left was a Communist Cuban guard running beside the jeep, hands outstretched and reaching for me.

I balanced the steering wheel with my left knee, snatched the wire cutters from my belt, and rammed the 18 inches of steel behind me. The Cuban soldier fell, the wire cutters imbedded in his chest. I smiled as I stomped the clutch and up shifted, the jeep now speeding past the tents, the huts, and the angry shouting guards and their guns. I triggered another burst from the Schmeisser, hitting a man who looked like an officer. I hoped he was the camp commandant.

The Schmeisser was shot dry and I dropped it beside me on the front seat, snatching the worn blue Browning High Power into my right fist, thumbing back the hammer, and firing the first round into the face of a Cuban soldier who'd thrown himself up on the hood of the jeep. The soldier fell away; there was a scream as the jeep rolled over something. I didn't care what it was.

The High Power blazed in my right hand as I fought the wheel of the jeep with my left. I made a sharp left turn, the jeep almost flipping over as I gunned it forward. Holding the pistol awkwardly, I rammed the stick into third gear, the engine noise so loud I could barely hear the shouts now.

Two Cuban soldiers were running after me, the gate a hundred yards ahead. I rammed the Browning straight out with my right hand, fired once, and then once again; the nearer of the two Cubans threw his hands to his face as he fell. The second man, unhit, dove into the jeep, his hands reaching out for my throat. I tried bringing the gun up to fire but the man was in the way, his hands tightening as the jeep swerved out of control. I felt fear, fear that said I was going to die; then I felt rage and screamed, "No, I'm not!"

CHAPTER FORTY-SIX

I dropped the Browning and clawed at the Cuban's face. I got my fingers into the man's mouth by the left cheek and ripped as hard as I could. The man's face split on the left side; the fingers released from my throat and I grasped the 9mm pistol, snapping back the trigger. The muzzle was flush against the Communist soldier's chest as I jerked the trigger, a scream from the torn face ringing loud in my ears as he turned loose and fell back into the mud.

I cut the wheel right just in time, the left fender crashing into a row of packing crates that tumbled into the mud. The High Power still in my right fist, I cut the wheel harder right with less than fifty yards to go until I reached the main gate. A dozen guards stood by the gate shooting at me; I jammed the Browning High Power into my trouser band and fumbled on the seat for the Schmeisser. Clumsily, I changed sticks in the submachine gun, smacked back the bolt and brought the muzzle of the weapon up over the hood, my left fist locked on the wheel again. I held my fire.

The distance to the gate was now twenty-five yards; the guards at the gate were still shooting. I remembered what Rourke told me about practical firing range. I closed to fifteen yards and began pumping the trigger in two-round bursts, this time firing at the greatest concentration of the guards. One man went down, then another. The guards ran as the jeep rammed toward them.

I kept a steady stream of two-round bursts, nailing another guard. I jammed the gas pedal to the floor as the jeep homed in on the gate and shouted, "Now!" The front end of the vehicle crashed against the wood and barbed wire gate, shattering it. The jeep stuttered a moment then pushed ahead. I brought the SMG back up, firing it out as I cut the wheel into a sharp right onto the road.

As I sped past the concentration camp, the noise from behind me had all but stopped. I looked to the right, toward the camp. I could see men, women, and children. I imagined I saw the old man with the festering leg wound who had told me so much, and the young woman with the dead baby. Tears filled my eyes but I told myself it was the wind of the slipstream around the vehicle doing it to my eyes. Every person in the camp compound was waving their arms in the air, cheering. Don't ask me how I felt at that moment. Truthfully, I have never been able to put it into words.

CHAPTER FORTY-SEVEN

"I don't know what the hell you're talkin' about, fella," the red-faced, beer-bellied man told me then turned back to work on his boat.

I told him, "A Captain Reed gave me your name, Tolliver. He said you were the man down here."

"I don't know a Captain Reed; now get out of here!"

The sun glared down on me, my legs tensed; I realized I'd been balling my fists. I reached out with my left hand and grabbed the florid-faced Tolliver by the left shoulder and spun him around. My right fist flashed out and caught the larger man at the base of the chin, the man falling back across the front of his boat.

Tolliver pushed himself up onto his elbows, squinting at me. "Who the hell are you, boy?"

"I told you, my name is Paul Rubenstein. I'm just a guy who needs your help. I know Captain Reed of U.S. II," the term Rourke was now using for our new government. "He was on a fast track with the military before the Night of the War. Currently, he is the coordinator for all Resistance activities in this area, usually has a bent stem Sherlock Homes pipe clenched in his teeth but rarely, if ever, lights it. He and my partner have coordinated on several missions since the start of this insanity. He gave me your name when I told him I was coming down here. Now you're bigger than I am, probably stronger, but believe me I can be meaner. I've learned how since the Night of the War. Now," I shouted, "I need your help!"

"Doin' what?"

"You ever go down by the camp, the big one?" I asked.

"Maybe."

"I'm going to break everybody out of there—and you're going to help me," I said.

"You're full of shit, boy."

I glanced over my shoulder, saw no one by the sandy cove where I'd found Tolliver working on his beached boat. Then, I reached under my jacket and pulled out the Browning High Power, shoving the muzzle less than two inches from Tolliver's nose. The hammer went back with an audible double-click. I said with a coldness I had never felt before, "If you can sleep nights seeing those people in there, then whatever I could do to you would be a favor. You either help me round up some people in the Resistance to get those folks out of there, or I'm killing you where you stand."

"You're the one caused all that fracas there this morning, ain't you?"

I nodded and said, "Yeah, I am."

"Put the gun away. Why the hell didn't you say so in the first place? I'll help and then we can all get ourselves killed together. Never fancied much dying alone, if you get my drift."

I raised the safety on the Browning and started to shift it down when there was a blur in front of my eyes. Tolliver's right fist moved, and I fell back into the sand. Tolliver grabbed for his gun. "Now take it easy, fella. That was just to make us even. You shoot me and you'll never find the Resistance people." Tolliver's big florid face creased into a smile and he stuck out his right hand. Rubbing my jaw with my left hand, I looked at the bigger man and then we both started to laugh.

CHAPTER FORTY-EIGHT

I looked across the hood of the jeep then at Tolliver beside me, behind the wheel. I told him it was a death camp, as I stared past the hood of the jeep to the lower ground, the road and the camp beyond it. He then told me the commandant had a reputation for being anti-Jewish and they put an anti-Semite in charge of a detention camp in an area with a large Jewish population. I interrupted him and told him that they know what is going on, the Communist Cuban Government.

He told me that some were saying that the commandant, Captain Gutierrez, disliked the Jews almost as much as the anti-Castro Cubans and that he'd been exterminating every one of them he could find.

I asked him why he's waited so long to do something. He told me to just to keep looking and I'd see for myself. He pointed over his shoulder. With my palms sweating, I turned around and looked behind the jeep. Tolliver's number one man, Pedro Garcia, a free Cuban, had gone to get the rest of the Resistance force. My heart sank; there were two men about my age, a woman of about twenty, and a boy only sixteen. Tolliver, his voice lower than mine, sighed hard. "That's why, Rubenstein. Two men, a woman, a boy, me, and Pedro, that's it. Now you. You still want to do this thing?"

I turned around in the jeep's front passenger seat, staring down over the hood toward the camp. "Hell yes," I rasped, the steadiness of my own voice surprising me. "Yes I do."

I felt the ground shaking and looked at Tolliver. He told me little quakes like that had been coming the last week or so. He didn't know why because the area was not earthquake country.

The trembling in the ground stopped, and I told him that we'd work out the details and get started. Then Tolliver asked me, "We're gonna wait until dark, right?" I thought a moment. I'd learned from Rourke to listen to the vibes, or my own senses, sometimes in the face of other evidence, and do what they added up to.

I told him no, that we'd go in the daylight because they wouldn't expect an assault in the daylight. I just didn't think we had the time to wait. I told him we'd go soon. As I continued watching the camp, I wondered how soon was soon enough.

Tolliver dropped to the ground behind a palm trunk, snapping, "What the hell is going on down there?" I dropped down beside him, the Schmeisser in my right hand. "It looks like they're getting out of the camp, but why? What's going on?"

My eyes were riveted to the camp. The guards were running from their posts; the officers were running too. I looked overhead. Planes of every description imaginable were filling the sky from the west. "Those are American planes!"

"Commies use ones they found on the ground a lot."

"No," I said. "They're coming from the west, maybe Texas or Louisiana."

"You're dreaming' kid," Tolliver snapped.

"No! Look—more of them!" The droning sound in the air was as loud as anything I could ever recall having heard. The sky was filled, the ground darkening under the shadows of the aircraft. The ground began to tremble under me, but this time more violently than before. I stood up, Tolliver trying to pull me down; I shook away Tolliver's hand. "It's an earthquake. Some of those planes are landing." I looked down toward the camp. The Cuban guards and officers were fleeing, the gates of the compound wide open. "They're evacuating. There's gonna be an earthquake."

"You're nuts, kid."

I looked down to Tolliver and started to say something but then the ground shook hard. I jumped away as a crack eighteen inches wide began splitting across the ground, a palm tree fell, just missing Pedro Garcia and the other Resistance people.

"A damned earthquake!" As if to underscore Tolliver's shout, the ground began shaking harder; I fell to the dirt on my hands and knees.

"Oh my God!" I said. Time has a funny way of slowing down in a crisis; it happened now. I started to pray, I thought about the many times my parents had prayed. How I wished I could remember how to pray like my dad. I hadn't prayed in a long time. How I wished I was with them, praying as a family again. Long forgotten words tumbled from my lips, "Barukh ata Adonai Eloheinu, melekh ha'olam... Blessed are You, LORD our God, King of the universe. Barukh ata Adonai Eloheinu, Melekh ha'olam, asher kid'shanu b'mitzvotav v'tzivanu l'hadlik ner shel Shabbat. Blessed are You, LORD our God, King of the universe, Who has sanctified us with His commandments and commanded us to light the Shabbat candles." I didn't have candles but I hoped God would understand.

CHAPTER FORTY-NINE

I heard the sound of a low-flying plane and, looking up, found it in the sky. I looked down at the ground below the plane; there were cracks in the ground, widening it seemed by the instant. Rain began falling in sheets and I silently prayed for the pilot. With Tolliver, Pedro Garcia, and the others, we had moved and fought all the way to the airport. The other camps spilled open as their Cuban Communist guards and warders had fled for their lives. Hundreds of men, women, and children were freed.

Many of the Cuban troops had fled by boat; the crafts visible as I and the others had moved along the highway. Then, I dropped off, going over land to retrieve my Harley, cutting back to the road again just ahead of the comparatively slow going convoy of every sort of land vehicle imaginable. Men hung on the outsides of the trucks, riding on the hoods of the cars and on the roof tops. It had taken two hours to reach the airport, and the airport itself was the greatest scene of mass confusion I had ever witnessed. The noise was incredible, humans in total disorder, engines screaming from vehicles and airplanes, not to mention the yells and screams of people trying to escape the tremors and pounding rain.

Cuban planes were loading soldiers, Soviet and American planes loading refugees and people from the camps. The ground's trembling had been incessant, the cracks appearing everywhere in the runway surfaces. Then I spotted a Captain with the name "Reed" on his name tag, working to load one of the American planes impressed into the evacuation. I threaded my bike across the runways and buttonholed Reed, demanding to know what was happening. When Reed told me, my heart sank.

Jerry Ahern, Sharon Ahern and Bob Anderson

He told me that the tremors were the beginning of one massive quake that would cause the entire Florida Peninsula to separate from the rest of the Continental United States, what was left of it at least.

I nearly throttled Reed, demanding some kind of plane to get me to Miami where my parents were. Then I found out that Rourke and some woman seismologist who had first brought the news of the impending disaster had gone to Miami to convince the Cuban commander of the reality of the impending disaster. Although Reed assumed they had been successful since the evacuation had been ordered, there had been no word from him since.

Again, I demanded a plane. Reed finally agreed. There was a six passenger Beechcraft Baron specially altered to add nearly another fifty miles per hour to its airspeed, the plane Reed himself had arrived in. We loaded up and I watched as the ground cracked below the plane. The pilot manipulated the controls and we watched the sheets of rain slamming into the broken tarmac. I wondered if by the time we reached Miami there would be a Miami to reach.

During the flight I started thinking about if Rourke died and I somehow survived, I would be honor bound to continue the search for Rourke's wife and the two children. I wondered what I'd do when the plane landed—that is if we could land. Would I offload the Harley the pilot had grudgingly helped me get aboard? Would I somehow be able to find my parents, John Rourke, or Natalia—but then simply die with them as the earthquake continued and the entire peninsula went under the waves?

A chill ran up my spine. It would be better to die than to live and never have tried to rescue the people. I stopped, a smile crossing my lips as I pushed my wire-framed glasses up on the bridge of my nose. "The people I love," I murmured softly.

CHAPTER FIFTY

When we finally landed, the place was falling apart. The passenger door over the starboard wing opened. The first person I saw was John; he was shouting, "Paul! Paul!" I climbed down from the wing, running across the field toward him. As we met, Rourke sank forward; I managed to grab him just before he fell.

"John! Thank God it's you!"

"Paul, what the hell are you doing here?"

"My parents, John, I've gotta find them."

"They may have gotten out already," Rourke gasped.

"I've gotta know, John!"

Rourke just nodded, getting to his feet again. "I've got to get Natalia and an older man and his wife out."

"What?" I said.

"There!" Rourke pointed behind me. The ground was starting to break up now, the runway buckling in huge chunks. I didn't say anything. I ran across the airfield, jumping the cracks toward Natalia and the white-haired man and his wife. I stood there, the rain pouring down on me and the wind rising so that I could barely stand erect against it. Then I really started to run. I swept the older woman into my arms, kissing her; John watched as the white-haired man hugged me.

Natalia stepped back; then a smile came to her lips. John stopped running, "Jesus," he whispered. Somehow, out of all the refugees, the old man with the full shock of white hair and the woman with him were my mother and father.

Natalia was there; she kissed John's cheek. He spotted my motorcycle on the plane and whipped out his knife, cutting away the gear strapped to it. He rolled it toward the door. He shouted out to me, "Get you a new one, buddy! Can't take the weight right now!"

"Right!" I helped Rourke offload the bike. In moments, Natalia had gotten my mother and father aboard the plane. I was the last to board. Rourke shouted to the pilot, "Get this thing going!"

"We'll never get out of here," the pilot shouted. Rourke climbed forward, looking over the man's shoulder. The runway was starting to split down the middle, the rain pouring down more heavily, and the wind sock on the control tower that showed wind direction was spinning maddeningly. The ground was shaking beneath the plane. At the far edge of the field, Rourke could see a wall of water rising as a huge section of runway slipped across the beach area into the ocean. "Bullshit!"

Rourke shoved the pilot out of the way and slipped behind the controls. The pilot jumped down the access ladder and ran for his life. John shouted, "Paul, get in here as co-pilot!"

"I can't fly."

"I'll teach you; you'll love it!" Rourke shouted, throttling up the portside engine then the starboard. Rourke touched his fingers to his lips then to the control wheel. "Hang on! Here we go." Rourke started the plane across what was left of the runway, zigzagging despite the wind and trying to find a space clear enough of the massive, ever-widening cracks for a take-off.

"All right, now or never!" Rourke shouted. To our right beyond the tip of the starboard wing, there was a massive, thundering wall of water rising up, a tsunami—it must have been eighty feet high. The entire airfield started to come apart and fall into the ocean. Suddenly, the thunder ceased, at least in the plane.

CHAPTER FIFTY-ONE

John throttled out and the plane lurched ahead, pumping over a crack in the runway and settling down on the runway surface again. He glanced to his right; the water was rushing toward them, the runway half submerged, and waves started to slosh in front of the aircraft. "Now!" Rourke shouted. Pulling up and throttling out, the plane rose unsteadily. Water rushed across the runway as it dropped off below us. I wanted to turn around to see my parents and Natalia for perhaps the last time, but my eyes were riveted to the scene playing out ahead of me. I held my breath.

The control tower loomed up ahead. John fought the controls, working the ailerons and trying to bank the plane to starboard to miss the control tower with the portside wing tip. The accumulated G-forces were incredible; I had to help him pull the yoke. "Pray!" He shouted, seeing the control tower drop off to his left, the building already starting to collapse. As Rourke leveled off the twin Beechcraft, he looked down. Where there had seconds before been an airport runway, now there was ocean, waves surging as far as I could see.

CHAPTER FIFTY-TWO

When we landed the Beechcraft, the plane was almost out of fuel. As best I'd been able to judge from the maps, we were about twenty-five miles from President Chambers and U.S. II headquarters. And, it was raining. I sat in the plane, talking to Mom and Dad.

Outside, Natalia stood next to John; I don't know what they were talking about, but I had my suspicions. Later, I asked John, "Where do you plan to go next?"

"The Carolinas, maybe Georgia by Savannah. She was likely headed that way." President Chambers had ordered our plane to be refueled. The rest of the flight was a particular troubling time for me. Mom and Dad, wrapped in each other's arms, slept; this phase of their hell over. I sat more or less alone. Even though everybody else was just inches from me, I was sequestered in my thoughts, again. My questions kept coming and I was struggling to make sense of what the world and I had become and, more importantly, were becoming.

My world, the one I grew up in, was shattered; it was like the mirror I had looked in all of my life for direction. My very existence had been broken into a million pieces, and they were scattered all over the floor. The frame of the mirror was still there, but it was empty. I seemed to be constantly passing that empty frame. Out of habit I kept glancing at it, wanting to check if my hair was in place, if I had a spot on my shirt, or if a bird had managed to poop on my shoulder—but there was no reflection. Physically, I was in the best shape of my life. Emotionally, I knew I was a wreck.

John Rourke, on the other hand, seemed unaffected by everything that had happened. No, unaffected was not the correct word, uneffected was more accurate. Thinking back to our days on the motorcycles before all of this happened, I remembered a conversation John and I had; I had come up with a lot of questions during my "times to think" as I had started recalling our extended motorcycle journey. "John," I asked him once. "Aren't you ever afraid?"

We were taking a break and a leak on the side of the road. He had just fired up one of his cigars and he turned away from me, staring out at the horizon for a long time. When he turned back, he squatted in the dirt and said, "Sit down, Paul." I did.

"First of all, yes, I feel fear. In fact, all of the things I have feared would happen for so long have happened. Fear to me is a friend however. Being fearful means I'm thinking of what could happen. Fear is a good thing; it keeps you from being stupid and reckless."

"John," I said in disbelief, "you are the most reckless man I have ever met. You walk headlong into situations and battles and come out unscathed."

He smiled, "That my friend is because I think about things BEFORE I go into them. I can fear the potential outcome and I try to plan ahead to overcome the obstacles, the challenges, and the threats. I don't gamble Paul. I have never understood gambling. It makes no sense to me. In the old days, I had a friend who would gamble. He lost tens of thousands of dollars but every now and then, he won just enough back that it reinforced his need to gamble. I, on the other hand, like to think I take calculated risks. I see what could happen, I weigh the odds, I know my strengths but more importantly, I know my weaknesses. Then, I will act."

"But, you never show fear?"

"The fact I don't show it doesn't mean I don't feel it." He smiled and took another drag off the cigar, exhaling slowly. "Take you and me," he finally said. "What would you do if you saw me in a panic mode?"

"Hell," I said. "I'd panic also."

"Exactly," he said, "why should I let my own fear leech over to you? It could mean the difference in your own survival, not to mention mine."

"How do you do it? If you feel fear, if you see all that could happen, why don't you just walk away, go a different route or take another alternative?"

"Because," he said standing, "we're out of alternatives; I can't just walk away— all of this has been forced on us. We didn't create this mess. All of my life, I have tried to prevent it. There are times to watch, listen, and learn—then, there are times when decisive action is required and required right then. I've trained all of my life to know the difference."

"But how do you not show fear? Sometimes, it feels like my own fear has a death grip on me..."

"But you act anyway; you push through that fear," he said. "You're developing something it took me a long time to master."

"What the hell would that be?" I asked.

Rourke stood up, flipped the cigar away, walked to his motorcycle, and climbed on, starting the motor. As he slipped the transmission into first and started to drive off, he shouted over his shoulder one word and drove off, "Grace!"

CHAPTER FIFTY-THREE

All during the next phase of our journey, I reflected. The loss was terrible but I didn't know it at the time. I never saw my mom and dad again, except in my dreams and my memories. I hoped that when their time came, my Dad wrapped his arms around mom and said simply, "Shalom, I love you." At least that is what I had chosen to believe—that has been the source of whatever peace I found. I learned later that was not the way it happened at all.

*****

When we eventually landed, the next phase was about to start. True to his word, John replaced the Harley he had dumped out of the plane. Our motorcycles were off-loaded, and I sat there for a moment before I kicked my bike into gear and followed him. "Grace," what a strange word to come from the mouth of a man like John Rourke. Yet, the more I thought about it, it made perfect sense he would use that word. I thought of the Englishman, John Newton, once the captain of a slave ship, a lost soul who had an encounter with God during a violent storm at sea and became an ordained minister in the Church of England.

It started in my brain and then I hummed it. By the time I was five miles down the road, I was singing at the top of my voice, "Amazing grace! How sweet the sound that saved a wretch like me. I once was lost, but now am found; was blind, but now I see. T'was grace that taught my heart to fear, and grace my fears relieved. How precious did that grace appear the hour I first believed. Through many dangers, toils, and snares, I have already come; t'is grace hath brought me safe thus far, and grace will lead me home..."

Yeah, I know... you're thinking...strange song for a Jewish boy to be singing.

My Reflections:

Trusting your gut... This concept may not make much sense to you, it didn't to me in the beginning either. John described it to me as listening to the vibes, your own senses and doing what they said, even when it flew in the face of everything else. I guess it really is intuition. Sometimes that is all you have left when there is nothing else left that you trust, or everything you know is ripped from you and doesn't exist any longer.

The feelings of loss and uncertainty kept knocking on the doors of my consciousness. I didn't answer that door. I did not know what I was becoming; killer, manic... what? Yet, at the end of each episode, each battle, each question... I was finding answers and blessings.

Question: Would I find my mother and father again?

Blessing: I was still able to search.

Question: Why did John never show fear?

Blessing: Learning that feeling fear and showing it were not the same things. The difference was something called Grace, such a simple uncomplicated thing.

PART V

CAUGHT IN THE WEB

CHAPTER FIFTY-FOUR

Things shifted in our universe. How quickly things change; how quickly good deeds are forgotten and unreasoned—or reasoned. Hatred springs back from the depths of human nature to take control. Just three days prior, Natalia had been rescuing wives and babies. But now, none of that mattered. She was Russian and the Russians had started World War III, destroyed much of the United States, and invaded American shores. Natalia was Russian. It didn't matter who she was, just what.

I was framed in the open cargo bay, pushing my glasses back off the bridge of my nose as I shouted, "John, what the hell..." Two pickup trucks were closing fast, gunfire now being leveled at him from the beds of the trucks. The West Coast mirror on the right-hand side of the vintage Ford pickup Rourke drove exploded. John snatched at one of the twin Detonics stainless .45s he carried in the double Alessi shoulder rig. He aimed the pistol as his thumb cocked the hammer. He turned his face away from the passenger-side window, firing as the shattering outward of the passenger-side glass, and the roar of the 185-grain JHP in the confined space all came together, I'm sure making his ears ring.

I watched as John looked toward the passenger side; the nearest of the two trucks swung away. He glanced to his left, seeing the pursuing mob. The mob split, a wing of it running diagonally from the access road toward the field to cut him off or to reach the airplane ahead of him. Natalia's face, her brilliantly blue eyes framed in the bell of her almost black and past shoulder-length hair, was visible through the pilot's side storm window.

Rourke skidded to a stop behind the left wing and hollered, "Paul, get everything nailed down fast, if it isn't already." Without another word, Rourke ran toward the wing stem and jumped for it, the pilot's side door opening under his right hand. Natalia was seated behind the controls.

"Move over," Rourke ordered her. She slipped out of the pilot's seat as Rourke slid down behind the controls. He checked the parking brake. "You through preflighting?"

"Yes," Natalia responded, sounding lifeless. "Everything's fine; ready?" He didn't say anything. Through the pilot's side storm window at least three dozen armed men were running across the field; and one of the trucks, a Chevy, was rolling again. "Damnit," he rasped to himself and then hollered to me, "Paul! Get that cargo hold buttoned up! Then get up here with a gun!"

"You can't ask him to shoot those people for me," I heard Natalia say in a whisper, as I started back. Not looking at her as he spoke, Rourke ran a visual check of the avionics. "You listen to me and good. Russian or whatever, I don't even have the words for it. Maybe Paul does. But the three of us, we've come this far together. And that means something." Rourke checked the oxygen. The cowl flap switches were open. He set the fuel selector valves to "main," the induction air system to "filtered."

He surveyed the control panels; there wasn't time for a full check. He flipped some things and the props started turning, way too slowly. "Paul, bring your gun!" he throttled out. Turning to Natalia he said, "Little late to ask but are the wheel chocks gone?"

"Yes." She smiled, laughing for an instant. Rourke nodded, the mob less than a hundred yards away now and the Chevy closing fast. There was no glass in its windshield, and men packed in its truck bed were firing rifles and shotguns. "Paul!"

"Right here," I shouted.

John glanced at me; I had his CAR-15 in my right hand. "Put a few shots out the storm window," Rourke ordered. Then, concentrating on getting airborne, he ignored the mob. He released the parking brake. "Let's get the hell out of here. Brace yourself Paul and keep shooting." Pieces of hot brass pelted John's neck and shoulders from me firing the Colt assault rifle toward the mob from almost directly behind him.

Rourke rasped half to himself, "Full throttle. God helps us." He released the brake. The aircraft was already accelerating. Rourke ordered me to buckle up. More of the hot brass pelted him and then suddenly stopped as my magazine emptied. Above the roaring of the engines there were now sounds of gunfire from the field of projectiles pinging against the aircraft fuselage.

"What if they hit something?" I called out.

"Then we maybe die," Rourke answered emotionlessly. He checked his speed; through the cockpit windshield, the runway was blurring under him now. The Chevy still came with gunfire pouring from it, the mob suddenly far behind. The pickup was closing fast. I could tell we didn't quite have airspeed yet. The far chain-link fence at the end of the airfield was coming up fast, too fast. More gunfire continued; the pilot's side window spider webbed beside Rourke's head as a bullet impacted against the glass. I kept firing, ignoring John's order to strap in. The Chevy swerved; one of the men in the truck bed fell out onto the runway surface.

The gunfire was heavier now, sparks flying as my slugs hammered against the pickup truck's body. "Hang on!" Rourke said as he worked the throttles to maximum and started to pull up—100 yards, 50 yards, 25 yards, and the nose started up. Rourke punched the landing gear retraction switch and as we cleared the fence top, the pelting of hot brass against his neck subsided, my gunfire having ceased.

"Thank God." I sighed.

John was working, trying to climb with gunfire still echoing from below and behind him. The airspeed was rising as he banked the aircraft hard to port. Natalia leaned half-out of her seat, across his right shoulder, me to his left. The Chevy, now far below us, had stopped. The men with rifles and shotguns in the pickup's bed were now minuscule specks, more a curiosity than a threat.

I plopped down in a seat, remembering to change magazines and safe the weapon. I had seen something that to the Paul Rubenstein I used to be, would have never made sense. To the man I was now, it did make sense. No, it wasn't that it made sense, it was that it was understandable. Mankind has an innate capacity for beauty, good, and greatness. But there is an animal intellect that civilization simply puts a bridle on. When that bridle is removed, a snorting, slobbering beast is released. That was what I had just witnessed; the old Paul would have found it incomprehensible.

The new Paul understood, primarily because I now knew I had that same snorting, slobbering beast in me. Could I keep the bridle on it, or would I succumb to the passion, rage, and vengeance I now felt in me? It was a sobering thought to say the least.

CHAPTER FIFTY-FIVE

"Can I breathe now?" I asked. Smiling, Rourke checked the oxygen system on the control panel then nodded.

"Yeah." He decided to breathe too... Natalia came with me to help resecure some of the gear that had jarred loose during the overly rapid takeoff. Below us was the expanse of wasteland that had once been the Mississippi Delta region. Now, like the rest of the Mississippi Valley from where New Orleans had been to its farthest extent north, the ground was a radioactive desert.

All of this had started The Night of the War. The angry mob of men and women at the airfield, the reluctance of Reed to risk an American life to save a Russian life, regardless of how valuable... it all started The Night of the War. The global fencing, the saber rattling, had ended long before anyone had realized and the nuclear weapons had been unsheathed and ready. Then they were unleashed, again by accident, a misstep, a miscalculation or according to some plan; it no longer mattered, that was now history.

The death toll was in the millions and the ground below was an irradiated vastness that would be uninhabitable for perhaps as long as a quarter-million years. The San Andreas Fault Line had brought about the feared mega quakes but far worse than anyone, save the wildest speculator, had ever imagined. Much of California and the West Coast had fallen into the sea, more millions of deaths.

The Soviet Army, the Soviet Union itself had to be nearly as crippled as was what had been the United States. The invading Soviet Army, headquartered in neutron-bombed Chicago, had set up outposts in surviving major American cities as well as industrial and agricultural regions, outposts that not only contended with the growing wave of American resistance, but with the brigand problem. Rourke smiled as he exhaled the gray smoke of his cigar. "It all has something in common with the ancient conquerors, the brigand warfare, the pillaging, and the slaughters," he said. For it was after the war that both the best and worst of humanity had risen to the foreground. For me, a young Jewish New Yorker who had never ridden anything more challenging than a taxi and had never fought anything tougher than an editorial deadline; it had been both an exhilarating and devastating transformation.

Now, in the few short... what had it been? Sometimes it seemed like years but weeks more probably. Whatever it had been since the world had forever changed, I had forever changed as well. I had toughened up; I was good with a gun and as at home on a motorcycle as I had been in a desk chair. Even in the short period of time that had elapsed, the wonder and excitement were there as had been from the first, with each new challenge; but there was something else. A pride, a determination derived just from having survived, from having fought, and from having surmounted obstacles.

I had grown to be the best friend Rourke told me he ever had, like a brother. I had never been blessed with a natural brother but now, at last, I had one. Then there was Natalia; Rourke had first met her before the war. John had been a CIA covert operations officer in Latin America where she was working for her husband, Vladimir Karamatsov. Karamatsov worked for the KGB, the Soviet Committee for State Security and Natalia was one of his, Karamatsov's, agents.

Then, after the war, there was the staggering coincidence of finding her dying and wandering the West Texas desert; herself the victim of brigand attack. The feelings had grown between John and the Russian woman, despite her loyalty to her country, and despite her job in the KGB and despite her uncle, General Varakov, who was the Supreme Soviet Commander for the North American Army of Occupation. "Crazy," I murmured to myself.

Rourke had been pursuing the trail of his wife Sarah, and the children lost to him on the Night of the War. He met with a girl named Sissy, a research seismologist. She told him of the development of an artificial fault that resulted from the bombings. It could replicate the horror of the mega quakes that had destroyed the West Coast. This one however, would sever the Florida peninsula from the mainland. For all the destruction and the death, it had proven again that there still remained some humanity, some commonality of species. For with President Chambers of U.S. II and General Varakov, a Soviet-U.S. II truce had been struck to effect the evacuation of peninsular Florida in the hope of saving human lives. The job finished, the truce had ended and a state of war existed once again.

In our earlier conversations, John had told me he hadn't wanted to leave Sarah; he hadn't wanted to give the lecture in Canada on hypothermia, the effects of cold. The world situation had been already tense, but Sarah had insisted he go; she wanted some time to get herself repositioned emotionally and to try again with him.   While the two of us were in Canada, everything had simply and irrevocably gone to crap.

CHAPTER FIFTY-SIX

I didn't know it at the time, but below us was brewing another "bucket of crap," a massive winter storm system. It came on very fast. Rourke's knuckles were white, his fists bunched on the yoke now as the twin-engine cargo plane skimmed low over the icy roadway, the right engine hopelessly iced. The brakes held, but the plane started to skid as it hit the ice and snow-covered road. Rourke shouted and told us to get our heads down.

The plane was going out of control. He worked the flaps to decelerate, the brakes starting to slow him down as well now. John had lost total control; he shouted back at me, "Paul, we're bailing out! Get to the cargo door and jump for it; jump as far out as you can!" He grabbed Natalia, shoving her roughly ahead of him toward the fuselage door.

Then I realized I was stuck; my seat belt buckling mechanism had jammed. I told them to save themselves.

Rourke glanced toward Natalia; she was already working the handle on the cargo door with her left hand; in her right hand, something metallic gleamed, a knife. She reached the butt of it out to Rourke. Rourke snatched it from her hand, wheeling, the aircraft's lurching and bumping throwing him toward me. Collapsing against the fuselage, Rourke reached the knife blade under the webbing strap across my left shoulder, slicing it. Then he started for the leg strap, I could feel the rush of arctic-feeling air and hear the slipstream.

The fuselage door opened. Rourke's borrowed knife slashed apart the last of the restraints. The knife still in his right hand, he snatched at his CAR-15, yelling to me, "Jump for it, Paul—go on!" As Rourke was moving toward the door, I was already on my feet, the Schmeisser in my right hand; Natalia was starting to jump.

Fear clutched at me for a moment, a long moment as I dove out into the frigid air, ice spicules hitting me hard, and my body quickly numbing. Knowing I had no control as to where I would land, if I got that far, I closed my eyes and said a quick prayer. Before I had a chance to come to a meaningful segment of that prayer, I hit the ground, hard. Immediately, I did a body check to affirm that all parts were intact and able to move. I looked up just in time to see John heading downward, his leather bomber jacket in his hand as the out of control fuselage tail just missed his head.

I followed the plane's descent with my eyes for an instant then pushed myself to my feet, slipping on the ice, running, and lurching forward. I could see Natalia lying in the middle of the road; I was running toward her. I could hear the wrenching and groaning of metal. I wheeled, skidding on the heels of my black combat boots across the ice, watching as the plane crashed through the metal roadside barricade and disappeared over the side. We waited; there was no explosion but there wasn't much hope either.

There were three of us with only one jacket, a rifle and a submachine gun, neither of which had a spare magazine. We had a few pistols and a Bali-Song knife—that was it. Natalia was like a little girl after taking a spill on an ice rink. She sat with legs wide apart, her right hand propping her up and her left hand brushing the hair back from her face, hair already flecked with snow. I crouched beside her, as if waiting. John stopped walking, a yard or so from her still. He held up the knife. "Never told me about the Bali-Song knife."

She only smiled. Rourke glanced back where the plane had disappeared; if anything could be salvaged it would have to wait. The leather jacket was bunched in his left hand along with the CAR-15. He approached Natalia, squatted down beside her, and draped the coat across her shoulders. She was already shivering, as I was, and so was Rourke... "I've had the Bali-Song for a long time. Somehow you missed it when you found me in the desert. I don't know how but I made sure it was with me, just in case."

"Are you good with it?" Rourke asked her, shivering.

"Yes. If my hands weren't so cold, I could show you."

CHAPTER FIFTY-SEVEN

We had to get to the plane and retrieve our stuff; it wasn't easy. We were nearly frozen; John stuck his hands inside his trousers to thaw them out. When he was able to move his fingers, he withdrew them from inside his pants and then quickly started going through his things and our packs. With the pair of vintage, heavy leather Kombi ski gloves on his hands and a "seen-better-days" gray, woolen crewneck sweater on over his shirt, Rourke fed out part of the climbing rope from his pack; a rock secured to the free end.

"Stand back from the edge up there—got a chunk of rock on the end of this for weight!"

"Understood!" I shouted back. He started swinging the free end of the rope, the end weighted with the rock, feeding out more and more of the line. He made the toss and then we heard the sound of the rock slamming against something metallic—one of the supports for the guardrail perhaps?

On the fourth try, the weighted end of the rope held. "Paul, look for it!"

"I've got it, John."

Rourke nodded to himself and then shouted, "Secure it to something really sturdy; have Natalia help you!"

"It's set, John," Natalia's voice called down.

"Haul up on the rope; hurry up," Rourke called up. On the near end of the rope, he had our winter jackets secured. Later, Rourke huddled by the fire a few yards from the aircraft fuselage, the water nearly boiling, he was studying me. I had made it down the embankment quite well. It was not as professionally as Natalia had let herself down, but well nonetheless. The water in the pot was boiling and Rourke picked it up by the handle, his left hand still gloved and insulating his fingers and then he stood up.

John hated to but he had to; he kicked out the fire. The darkness was more real now as he started toward the glowing light of the Coleman lamp in the fuselage. The Space Blanket was wrapped around Natalia now, her coat being rather light for the extreme cold of the night. I knew John was chilled still, despite the fact that he had added the leather bomber-style jacket over his sweater.

I must have looked positively frozen to the bone. "Paul, why don't you fish through the gear and find a bottle of whiskey? I think we could all use a drink." Rourke smiled. I was up and moving as Rourke crouched down beside Natalia near the Coleman lamp.

Her gloved hands reaching for the pot of no-longer-boiling water, "You hold the food packets," she ordered.

"All right," Rourke murmured. There wasn't much of the Mountain House food left in his gear and he'd have to resupply once we got back to the Retreat. John called to me; I was still searching for the bottle. "Food's on, Paul."

I found a quart bottle of Seagram's Seven. "This bottle's cold; at least we won't need any ice, huh?" I laughed.

"Here, Paul." Natalia handed me the first of the three packs, the one with the hottest water added. I took the pack of beef stroganoff and settled down beside the Coleman lamp. "Like old times out there on the desert in Texas," I said, giving the food a final stir.

"John and I were just saying that," Natalia told him.

"This is good," I said through a mouthful of food. John broke the seal on the whiskey bottle, twisting open the cap and handing the bottle to Natalia. She smiled, putting the bottle to her lips and tilting her head back to let the liquid flow through the bottle's neck and into her mouth. John watched her intently. She handed him the bottle and, not wiping it, he touched the mouth of the bottle to his lips, taking a long swallow; then he passed the bottle to me.

"Sarah and the children couldn't make it across the Mississippi valley anyway—the radiation. So, I've gotta stop them—before they get into the fallout zone," John told us.

"If somehow we learn anything in Chicago, I will or my uncle will get word to you somehow," she said.

"I know that," Rourke answered.

"I hope you find them John, and they are safe and whole and that you can make a life for them. Somewhere."

"The Retreat," Rourke said emotionlessly. "The Retreat, only place safe. It's safe against anything except a direct hit; enough supplies to live for years, grow lights for the plants to replenish the oxygen, and that stream gives me electrical power. I can seal the place to make it airtight. But Sarah was right, it is just a cave. I don't know if I can see raising two children in a cave, even a cave with all the conveniences."

"You don't have any choice; you didn't start the war," she said, her voice suddenly guilt-tinged.

"Neither did you, Natalia. Neither did you," he murmured. She leaned tighter against him and he held her tighter.

"If things were different and we could be..." She didn't finish her thought. Rourke touched his lips to her forehead as he leaned back, her head on his shoulder. As he closed his eyes, he murmured the word that she hadn't said, "lovers." We both listened to the evenness of her breathing long past the time we should have fallen asleep... I was beginning to feel way outside of my own comfort zone, as if anyone else noticed.

CHAPTER FIFTY-EIGHT

It would be a long time before I understood why Natalia HAD to leave. She would later explain it this way, "I didn't want to leave, but I could not comprehend how I could stay. I was torn between my loyalty to my country and my disillusionment that had been building since meeting you and John. I was torn between my love of John and you also Paul, and my sincere belief that my only hope in saving both of you was to return and work to soften the impact of what my country had done. I thought, if I was successful, I could save both of you. I know that doesn't make sense to you but please try to understand... at that time, in those moments... it made sense to me."

My days, my whole life at this point seemed like a ride on a terrible rollercoaster traveling through a kaleidoscope while on steroids and LSD. No sooner did we survive one unsurvivable situation then the next terrible set of conditions slammed into us. The longer John delayed taking up the search, the closer Sarah and the children might get to the irradiated zone and the more chance there was that they would slip through his fingers. He wanted to catch up with them in the Carolinas; it was the only chance now.

New problem—without the plane, it would be impossible to drop off Natalia safely near Russian-dominated territory in northern Indiana. John's original plan had been to leave Natalia where she would be safe, then to drop me in Tennessee. He would then fly as close to Savannah as possible; he and I would try to catch Sarah and the children between us.

We came up with an alternate plan; I was to drop Natalia off. She would ride behind me on my bike. It had been a chore to remove our bikes from the crashed plane; luckily it was a controlled crash landing and they survived with just a few dings and scratches. The problem was getting them out of the cargo hold. Once that had been accomplished, it was a slow and laborious process getting them down from where the crash site was to the highway. Even after we got the bikes up onto the highway, the storm still showed no signs of abating.

CHAPTER FIFTY-NINE

The heart of the storm seemed to be to the south and west. With luck, she and I would be driving out of the storm, while he drove into it. John and I both still had Geiger counters. John would zigzag back and forth with his farthest range being the lower Carolinas.

I would leave Natalia in safe territory then travel back, retracing the route down from northern Indiana to Tennessee, then strike straight for Savannah from there. With luck one of us would intercept Sarah, Michael, and Annie. In two weeks, we were to rendezvous at the Retreat, hopefully one of us with Rourke's family in tow.

John started his bike, letting the engine warm up as he walked back toward us. My bike was already loaded and running. I started to say something but John cut me off. I wasn't certain why but urgency seemed now to obsess him.

"You memorized those strategic fuel supply locations so you can get gasoline?"

"Yes, yeah I did," I said.

"And take it real slow, really slow until you start getting out of this. Just be careful all the way, even after you gotten through the weather, a sudden temperature..."

"John, I'll do all right. Take it easy." I extended my gloved right hand and then pulled the glove away.

Rourke hesitated a moment then pulled off his own glove. "I know you will Paul; I know. I just... ahh..." Rourke simply shook his head, clamping his jaw tight. I knew he was wishing he had a cigar there to chew on.

"I'll walk you back to your motorcycle," Natalia said quietly, taking Rourke's bare right hand as soon as he released my grip.

"All right," Rourke answered her softly. "I'll see you Paul."

"Yeah, John. I'll be right behind you real soon." I let the bike warm up a bit and watched the two of them. John simply nodded then started back toward his machine. He looked at her once then looked away. One of his big bandanna handkerchiefs was tied over her head to cover her ears; I'm sure John's own ears were freezing. It was blue, making the blueness of her eyes even bluer. The sleeping bag bound around her made her figure virtually vanish under it. As they stopped beside his Harley, still within earshot (though I wasn't trying to eavesdrop), Natalia placed her hand on his face as he turned to her. "I love you, John Rourke. I'll always love you. Forever." She kissed his mouth hard.

She turned and ran away, almost slipping once on the ice; John watched her. She clambered aboard my bike and didn't look back as I gunned the machine, shot a wave over my shoulder, and started off. Natalia Anastasia Tiemerovna hugged her arms tightly around me; I knew she thought of me as a brother, as did John. She held on to me in order to stay aboard the slowly moving motorcycle, for the warmth my body radiated, and to give me the warmth of her body.

It had been three hours and the ice and snow had allowed us not more than a hundred miles, perhaps less. "Do you think the storm will intensify as John heads south?" she asked. I didn't answer and she repeated the question, louder. "Do you think the storm will intensify as John goes south, Paul?"

Turning slightly, I said, "I think so. May be slacking up a little soon for us, looks like it up..."

"Paul!" It was the first time I'd turned my face toward her in more than an hour. My eyebrows were crusted over with ice, my face red and raw to the point of bleeding on my cheeks. She ordered me to stop the bike. She suddenly realized that, while my body had shielded hers from the wind, my face had nothing to protect it.

"You let me drive," she said, dismounting. I looked at her, my eyes tearing from the wind but smiling despite it. "If I let anything happen to your face, well aside from the fact John would never forgive me, I wouldn't forgive myself," I told her. She threw her arms around my neck, hugging me a moment, then stepped back.

She had long ago resigned herself to John's chauvinism and liked it in her heart. I had every intention of treating her the same way. She pulled the blue and white bandanna from her hair. She started toward me saying, "Then you tie this over your face and stop for five minutes every half-hour, either that or I don't go another mile, Paul." She had decided that if I insisted on treating her like a woman then she could treat me like a little boy and impose her will on me. Selfishly I enjoyed it, even while feeling a little guilty for the pleasure of it. She bound the handkerchief at the back of my neck, pulling up the sides until the handkerchief covered all my face just below the eyes.

"You look very, very much like a bandit—a handsome bandit." She smiled.

I just shook my head and shrugged my shoulders. I didn't have time or the energy to talk; it was taking everything I had to keep the motorcycle upright on the ice, while the wind battered me. My face was numb and my hands were no better off. My knees and fronts of my legs were wet and cold. I didn't know how much longer I could do what I was doing, but there was nothing else I could do and no shelter to get out of this nasty weather. I had to slow down; my attention had to be focused or we'd go down. It stayed like that for what seemed like days, but it was only hours. Only hours...

CHAPTER SIXTY

When we stopped for the night, it was in the shelter of a bridge and she had bathed my face and massaged it as we huddled. When she woke me, she had one of the revolvers out of the holster. It and the one like it on her left hip were curious guns. On the right faces of their slab-sided barrels were engraved American Eagles. The guns were originally four-inch stainless steel Smith & Wesson Model 686s, the .357 Magnum L-frame.

On the left flats of the barrels were duplicate inscriptions: METALIFE INDUSTRIES, RENO, PA. BY RON MAHOVSKY. The revolvers were round-butted, polished, tuned, and perfect. Rourke, when they had been given to her by President Chambers, told her he had known the maker of the guns well before the Night of the War. They would be the best guns she would ever own.

Mahovsky had made the American Eagles for President Sam Chambers before the war and Chambers. For her part in the evacuation of Florida, he had insisted she take them. She smiled at the memory, recalling his words. "I can't very well give a Russian spy an American medal, can I? And anyway, we're fresh out of medals. Take these and use 'em to stay alive with, miss." She had taken them and the holsters Chambers had for them; Rourke had found her a belt that better matched her waist size.

She heard a noise. She extracted the second revolver now, gloves off and edging up to her feet. Natalia raised a finger to her lips then pointed to her ear. I was still half-asleep but I edged back from the fire, the battered Browning High Power coming into my right hand and the hammer slowly cocking back. In the stillness—against the wind, it sounded loud, too loud. She gestured to me with one of the guns that she would cross around behind the bridge support and look.

I nodded; I wore no boots but she did; there wasn't time for an alternate plan. The sleeping bag fell from her shoulders and she held the pistol in her left hand against her abdomen flat, to keep her coat closed more tightly about her. She shook her head; the wind caught her hair as she stepped out of the crude lean-to into the night. Brigands were her worry; Russian soldiers she could take care of. She had her identification, spoke Russian, and could prove who she was and lie about who I was. But brigands... that had been the risk we had run lighting a fire. Otherwise, my feet might have been gone. Frostbite, left untreated, could so quickly turn gangrenous.

She jerked when the noise came again; this time, not the noise of speech but the bolt of a weapon-assault rifle or submachine gun being opened. She stepped away from the bridge support, the glow of the fire glinting off the now two polished stainless steel revolvers in her fists. "What do you want?" she shouted.

One of the nearer assault rifle-armed figures turned toward her. "Ever'thin' you got, li'l gal." He laughed.

"You shouldn't laugh," she said calmly. The man wheeled the muzzle of his rifle toward her and both pistols bucked at once in her hands. The man's body hammered backward into the snow. The assault rifle discharged, its muzzle flashed, lighting up the night as the second nearer man started to turn to fire. She caught the sight of hair; it wasn't a man but a woman. Natalia fired the pistol in her left hand then the one in her right. The body of the woman twisted and contorted as it fell, her assault rifle impacting into the snow beside her.

Gunfire was coming from the other two, and Natalia dove for cover behind a pile of discarded sewer pipes to her left. I had already opened up with the Schmeisser. Then I got jumped; my right arm tangled up in the sling of the Schmeisser, my left hand holding back the knife of my opponent. I was fighting three guys at the same time. I dropped the Schmeisser, my right fist hammered up into the midsection of the vastly larger man. I missed my target and smashed my fist into his groin; it worked equally well. Come to think of it, it worked better. He crumpled to the dirt; I got my Schmeisser sling free and stitched three rounds into his face, swinging it up against the other two. Out of the eight rounds that poured out, I only missed with three. I was getting the hang of trigger control.

When it was over, she said, "Too bad."

"Yeah, what a waste of human life," I said.

170

"That too," she told me. "But with all the bullet holes, none of their coats will do us much good for added warmth." She started back toward the windbreak, saying, "Check that they're all dead, while I get my other gun and the knife. If any of them aren't dead, tell me," she added.

Automatically, she emptied the revolver of the spent cases and then reloaded it with one of the remaining Speedloaders. She loaded the second revolver as well, holstering both guns; and with her hands trembling, she lit a cigarette. "Tired!" she screamed.

I said simply, "We have to go. They probably have friends."

CHAPTER SIXTY-ONE

Settling my glasses back on the bridge of my nose, I pulled down the bandanna covering my face as I slowed the Harley, the snow under it slushy and wet. I looked up and for a brief instant, could see a patch of blue beyond the fast scudding gray clouds.

"It is breaking up," Natalia said from behind me.

"'Bout time." I smiled. I suddenly had the realization of the air temperature on my face. "Must be twenty degrees warmer than it was when we broke camp," I told her over my right shoulder.

"We should be getting into my territory soon. Paul, there may not be time," she began. "Pull over."

We came to a stop. "I know; give John your love, right?"

She punched me in the back. "Yes." I heard her laugh. "And, this is for you." I felt her hands roughly twisting my head around; her face bumped my glasses as she kissed me full on the lips. "I won't ask you to give that to John—that was for you." She smiled.

"Look, you don't have to... "

"To go back to my people? John and I went over that. I have to. I'm a Russian, no matter how good my English is and no matter how much I can sound or look like an American, I'm a Russian. What I feel for John, what I feel for you as my friend; that will never change. But, being what I am won't change either."

"You know you're fighting on the wrong side," I told her, suddenly not smiling.

"If I said the same thing to you, would you believe it? I don't mean believe that I believed it, but believe it inside you?"

"No," I said flatly.

"Then the same answer for you, Paul. No. My people have done a great deal of harm, but so have yours. With good men like my uncle, perhaps I can do something to..."

"Make the world safe for Communism?" I laughed. She laughed too, saying through her laughter, "You're not the same barefoot boy from the Big Apple I met long ago, Paul."

I was deadly serious when I said to her, "And you're not the same person you pretended to be. I'll tell you what your problem is. You grew up believing in one set of ideals, and you've been realizing what you believed in at that time was wrong. Karamatsov was the Communist, the embodiment of..."

"I won't listen anymore, Paul." She smiled touching her fingers to my lips.

"All right." I smiled, kissing her forehead as she leaned against my chest for a moment. "Just think what a team you and John would make," I told her then.

She looked up at me, her eyes wet. "Fighting? Always fighting? Brigands or some other enemies?"

"That's not what I meant. You can find other ways to be invincible together." I laughed because I'd sounded so serious, so philosophical.

"He, he can't. And I can't."

"What if he never finds Sarah?"

"He will," she told him flatly.

Again, I asked the question, "What if he never finds Sarah? Would you marry him?"

"That's none of your business, Paul," she said, then smiled.

"I know it isn't, but would you?"

"Yes," she said softly then started to fumble in her bag. She took out a cigarette and a lighter then plunged the tip of the cigarette into the flame with what looked to me like a vengeance. We sat in silence for a long time, me confused and frustrated and Natalia angry, confused, and frustrated.

*****

"Stay where you are. Raise your hands and you will not be harmed!" I looked ahead of us; a half dozen Russian soldiers, greatcoats stained with snow, and at their head a man I guessed was an officer. "You are under arrest. Lay down your arms!"

She spoke in English, I guessed so I could understand. "I am Major Natalia Tiemerovna..." I thought I detected her voice catch for an instant before she added, "of the Committee for State Security of the Soviet."

CHAPTER SIXTY-TWO

The story that Natalia concocted worked. The Russians believed I was one of the covert spies on my own mission and I was simply helping her. She said I was escorting her through American territory because I had posed as one of the Resistance and was known to the Resistance people operating the area. My stomach churned, but I had agreed and backed up her story.

Natalia's credentials were checked and I was released. We had shaken hands only, but she had blown me a kiss by pursing her lips as we spoke a few yards from the Soviet troops. Then I boarded the bike and started back into the storm. I looked at her over my shoulder once; she hadn't waved, but I'd felt she would have if she could have.

*****

The rain was heavy and cold but not freezing. It dripped down inside the collar of my permanently borrowed Army field jacket; my hair was too wet to bother pulling up the hood. My gloves were sodden. The Schmeisser was wrapped in a ground cloth and the Browning High Power was under my jacket. My boots were wet, the Harley having splashed through inches-deep puddles in the road surface, and the going was slow to avoid a big splash that could drown the engine. I squinted through my rain-smeared glasses at the sign. Kentucky, I was entering Kentucky.

I wondered two things: would I ever see Natalia again now that she was safe with Russian troops and had John made it through the storm to find Sarah and the children yet? If Rourke had gotten through the storm at all wasn't something over which I worried. John was all but invincible, unstoppable. But, as I released the handlebar a moment to push my glasses up, I wondered, *Had John Rourke found them yet?*

Chapter Sixty-Three

I felt better and was making better time. The weather was almost warm again as I moved through Kentucky, nearing the Tennessee line, the Harley eating the miles since I had made the stop at the strategic fuel reserve John Rourke had told me about. There was slush, heavy slush, at the higher elevations. And in case the temperatures dropped with the evening, I wanted to get as far south as possible. If I pressed, I could get near the Georgia line and be well toward Savannah by nightfall.

By now, John should be crisscrossing the upper portion of the state and into the Carolinas, looking for Sarah and the children. Perhaps, I felt myself smile at the thought; perhaps he had already found them. Should I start for the Retreat? No, I should follow the plan. If John had designed it, it was...

I looked up; a helicopter, American, but with a Soviet star stenciled over it, was passing low along the highway, coming up fast behind me. "Holy shit!" I bent low over the machine, running out the Harley to full throttle. I had almost forgotten about the Russians, and what were they doing? "Joy Riding?" I snapped, releasing the handlebar a moment to push my wire-rimmed glasses back.

"Damnit!" The helicopter was directly above me, hovering. I started to reach for my pistol to fire but the machine pulled away, vanishing up ahead. I braked the Harley, glancing to my right; there was a dirt road, little more than a track. The helicopter was coming back toward me and I wrenched the bike into a hard right, sliding across the slushy highway toward the dirt road beyond and jumping the bike over a broad flat low rock. There was a loudspeaker sounding behind me.

"Paul Rubenstein. You are ordered to stop your machine. You are ordered to stop and lay down your arms. You will not be harmed."

I glanced skyward at the helicopter almost directly over me. The loudspeaker sounded again. "You will injure yourself if you pursue this course of action. We mean you no harm." The voice was heavily accented. "You are ordered to surrender!"

"Eat it!" I shouted up to the helicopter, the downdraft of the rotor blades making my voice come back to me. Ahead, I could see the second helicopter, hovering low, too low over the road where it widened. I could see uniformed troopers in the massive open doors of the formerly U.S. machine.

"Paul Rubenstein. This is by order of General Varakov; you are to stop immediately and lay down your arms." I spotted what Rourke had told me once was a deer trail; it looked the same. I wrenched the bike into a hard left onto the deer trail, the branches cracking against my face and body as I forced the machine through. The path was bumpier than the dirt road I had just left.

"Paul Rubenstein. You are ordered to..." I looked up, cursing under my breath and then looked ahead; a deadfall tree lay across the path. I started to brake but the Harley skidded from under me; I threw myself clear, hitting the ground hard. I pushed to my feet; the Harley was lost somewhere in the trees. I started running, snatching at the High Power under my jacket. I stopped at the tree line, snapping off two fast shots toward the nearest helicopter; the machine backed off. I lost sight of the other one after heading onto the deer path.

Machine gunfire was coming at me, hammering into the ground and the trees ten yards behind me as I ran; I swatted away the tree branches that snapped at my face. Pine boughs still laden with snow pelted me, washing wet snow across my face. The machine gunfire was edging closer and I dropped to my knees, wheeling, firing the High Power in rapid, two-shot semi-automatic bursts. The helicopter backed off.

"Son of a gun..." I smiled, pushing up to my feet and turning to run again. Three Russian soldiers blocked the path. The other helicopter, I realized, had landed its men. I started to bring the pistol on line to fire, but something hammered at the back of my neck. I fell forward, the gun dropping from my grip.

Hands reached down to me; voices spoke in Russian. I rolled onto my back, my left foot snapping up and out into the crotch of one of the Russians and the man doubled over. I reached up, snatching hold of a fistful of uniform, hauling myself up to my knees, and dragging the soldier down with my left fist smashing upward into his face. Then I was on my feet, running. Someone tackled me and I went down, the ground slapping hard against me. Another man was on top of me, holding me.

I snapped my left elbow back, found something hard against it and heard a moan and what sounded like a curse, despite the language barrier. I pushed myself up, wheeling my left fist swinging out and catching the tip of a chin. A man fell back under. I wheeled again and saw the two bunched together fists swinging toward me like a baseball bat. I felt the pain against the side of my neck and then there was nothing but darkness and a warm feeling.

CHAPTER SIXTY-FOUR

The man I would learn was Ishmael Varakov, stepped from the back of his limousine to walk across the airport runway surface. The V-STOL aircraft's engines were maddeningly loud; he looked like his feet ached and his belly felt constrained with his uniform blouse buttoned.

He walked toward a dark-blue Cadillac, stopping for an instant to glance once again at the V-STOL aircraft. He watched as the remainder of the cargo was put aboard, Natalia's things I later found out. He started walking again, stopping beside the rear door of the Cadillac; the driver, an Army Corporal, saluted. Varakov returned and the driver opened the rear door on the driver's side. As Varakov stepped inside, he looked at the man. "Go talk with my driver—about women or something." Varakov slammed the door shut behind him.

In the far corner of the back seat sat Natalia Tiemerovna. Next to her, between him and her, I sat. "What the hell do you want with me?" I demanded.

"Impertinent young man, aren't you?" Varakov smiled, "Here, if you promise not to shoot me with it yet." Varakov reached into his briefcase and took out my Browning High Power. Varakov rammed the magazine up the magazine well then snapped back the slide of the pistol. He lowered the hammer over the loaded chamber and handed the pistol to me. My hands had been opening and closing, balling in and out of fists.

"I told you," Natalia murmured. "My uncle is a man to trust... not to..."

I looked at her and she fell silent. Then I turned to Varakov. "What do you want, General?" I almost spat the last word.

"You don't like Russians. Let me guess but you like Natalia, my niece. Doesn't that strike you as odd young man?"

"I know her and..."

"You would be a terrible debater. It would then follow that once you got to know me, you would like me, wouldn't it? Logically, I mean?" Varakov smiled.

Natalia laughed.

"Well, will you listen to me young man? For I need your help. Natalia needs your help; she doesn't know it yet. She is leaving here—for an extended stay."

Natalia looked at him but only said, "Uncle?"

"I had Catherine pack your things; they are aboard that aircraft out there." Varakov gestured behind him. "Everything." Varakov looked at me then past me at Natalia.

"You are both so young. It is the young who always risk for the errors of the old, like me. I have learned something of paramount importance—to your friend John Rourke, something which I must discuss with John Rourke in person. It is of importance to him and..."

"I'm not bringing John into a trap," I snapped, my right fist tightening on the butt of the pistol I held.

"Two questions. Would Natalia knowingly do Rourke harm?"

"Of course not," I told him.

"And would I, if I were planning to deceive both my niece and Rourke, entrust Natalia to him through you? Obviously not. That is why she goes with you—for that reason and for her own safety."

"My safety..." Natalia began. "But..."

Varakov shushed her, "You asked no questions when I sent you to explore Rozhdestvenskiy's office."

"Roz, what?" I asked.

"Rozhdestvenskiy, a singularly good-looking fellow yet singularly unpleasant I am afraid." Varakov looked outside the window, watching his driver and the driver who had brought Natalia and me, talking; "I need you, Mr. Rubenstein, to take Natalia, my niece, to wherever it is John Rourke lives."

"The Re..." I started but stopped.

"The Retreat? Yes, I believe that's the place. Then..." Varakov said as he fished inside his case, "you will give him this message. I am also giving you papers of safe conduct, for yourself and for Rourke, but I cannot guarantee how long my orders in such matters will be strictly enforced."

"Uncle," Natalia began.

"Silence, child." He looked at Rubenstein. "Can I entrust to you, sir, the one thing in my own life I hold most dear, her life?" Varakov extended his hand.

I hesitated a moment, glanced at Natalia and then took Varakov's hand. "What the hell is going on here?"

"See? I told you that you would end up liking me, young man; I told you." He started out of the backseat, opening the door, Natalia's voice behind him as he exited the car.

"Uncle!" She ran around the back of the car then fell into his arms.

"I would not have let you go without saying goodbye, child. I will see you again. Do not fear."

"What is happening, Uncle Ishmael? What is that report of Rozhdestvenskiy, the Eden Project abstract?" I perked up on hearing that name; John had asked me about Eden.

"Be thankful you read no more of it. You will learn the details when you come back here with John Rourke. There is no other way."

"Come back here with…"

"You must, child and when Rourke reads the letter I have sent him, he will want to come. If he is the man I think he is… that you think he is… he is the only one." Varakov stepped back, holding his niece at arms' length. "You look lovely, a beautiful dress; is that coat real fur?"

"Yes." She looked down.

"I fear where you are going you'll have to change aboard the aircraft. I know little about survival retreats but I don't imagine one reaches them in high heels and silk stockings."

"They are nylon-silk stockings…"

"Yes. Nylon. Be careful." He folded his arms around her.

When we were on our way, I leaned close to Natalia and asked, "What is this Eden Project?" She just shook her head.

CHAPTER SIXTY-FIVE

We were dropped off along with my motorcycle at a point I had designated. We were only about fifty miles from the Retreat, but the Russians didn't know that. When they left, I brought the subject of the Eden Project up again. "Paul, honestly, I don't know. There are things just surfacing that I don't understand. My uncle is seriously concerned about something he wouldn't even share with me. I am as shocked as you are that he wants to speak directly to John. Paul, I'm worried." Then we climbed onto the bike and headed east.

When we had arrived at the coordinates, Natalia dismounted and placed her hands on her waist, just above the Safariland holsters carrying the twin Smith & Wesson revolvers. She looked at me, saying, "I don't see anything, Paul."

"You're not supposed to. When John brought me up here the first time, he told me that was the whole idea." I smiled in the gray predawn. "I can't really explain it as he does but I guess he did a lot of research. He said it was the way Egyptian tombs were sealed and things like that. He wanted the place tamper-proof. Watch this."

I approached a large boulder on my right and pushed against it, and the boulder rolled away. I walked to my left, pushing a similar but not identical boulder. It was more squared off. As I pushed, the rock on which Natalia stood beside began to drop down. As the rock beneath dropped, a slab of rock opened inward.

"John told me it's just a system of weights and counterbalances," I said. "Maybe you understand it better. Didn't you have some training as an engineer?"

"Nothing like this," she said, looking literally amazed. I shined a flashlight in the shaft of yellow light; she could see me bending over, flicking a switch. The interior beyond the moved-aside slab of rock was bathed in red light now. "All ready for Christmas." I laughed. "Red light? That was a joke."

"Yes, Paul," Natalia murmured.

"I'll get the bike. Hold this." I handed her the flashlight. She studied the rock; I brought the Harley Low Rider inside. "Now watch this," I said, suddenly beside her.

"Yes, Paul." She nodded, giving me back the flashlight. I moved over beside a light switch and then shifted a red-handled lever downward, locking it under a notch. I left the small cave for an instant, and she could both hear and see me rolling the rock counterbalances back in place outside. I returned to the red-handled lever, loosed it from the notch that had retained it and raised it. The granite slab, the door, started shifting back into place, blocking the entrance.

"What are those steel doors for?" Natalia asked, gesturing beyond the pale of red light.

"The entrance inside." I moved toward the doors then began working a combination dial, then another, all in the shaft of yellow light from the angle head. "John installed ultrasonic equipment to keep insects and critters out."

"And closed-circuit television," Natalia added, looking up toward the vaulted rock above her.

"Can you find that switch for the red light back there?" I asked her.

She nodded in the dim light and found the switch, turning it off. There was near total darkness now. "Paul?"

"I'm right here; wait a second." She heard the sounds of the steel doors opening. She stepped closer to the beam of the angle head flashlight, staring into the darkness beyond it. "Ya ready?" I asked.

"I don't know, for..." She heard the sound of a light switch clicking. She closed her eyes against the light a moment then opened them. "I don't believe it."

"That's the Great Room." She looked at me, watching the pride and happiness in my face.

"Great, yes," she repeated. She started to walk down the three low steps in front of her, a ramp to her left; her eyes were riveted on the waterfall and the pool it made at the far end of the cavern. Then she drifted to the couch, the tables, the chairs, the video recording equipment, the books that lined the walls, and the weapons cabinet.

And on the end table beside the sofa... She stopped, approaching the couch and picking up the picture frame there.

"Would you like a drink, Natalia?" I asked. "I can show the rest to you after a while."

"What? A drink, yes," she called back. The little boy in the photo, he was a miniature twin of John Rourke. "Michael," Natalia murmured, smiling. "So fine, so beautiful, so strong. And the little girl, the face of an imp," Natalia was smiling more broadly now. The smile faded, the next photo was John with his arm around a woman who looked about Natalia's age, maybe a little older. She was pretty with dark hair and green eyes, or so it seemed in the picture. "Sarah Rourke," Natalia murmured.

"That's them," I said. "I didn't ask what you wanted. Figured Seagram's Seven would be alright."

"Perfect. That's perfect, Paul."

"That's Sarah, Michael and Annie. I feel almost as though I know them." I laughed.

"Yes, Paul, so do I," Natalia said, putting the picture down on the end table. "So do I." She stopped talking, then I could tell what she was thinking, and she looked like she was going to cry and didn't want to.

Unbidden, a thought, a quote from George Eliot came to my mind, "There is no despair so absolute as that which comes with the first moments of our first great sorrow, when we have not yet known what it is to have suffered and be healed, to have despaired and have recovered hope." I don't believe I ever saw a soul before in absolute despair. I wanted to reach out to her. I wanted to hold her and comfort her; I stood stupidly still. After all, I'm not John Thomas Rourke, I thought.

My Reflection:

No, I wasn't John Rourke. He had been my teacher, my brother, my salvation; without him I would have died countless times already. But for the first time since we had met, I was glad I was not him.

I can't say I was happy being me, but I was closer to feeling comfortable in my own skin than I had ever been. I had quit counting the "grow up moments." Yes, one day there might be Peace in the Valley; I actually believed that but not today and certainly not tomorrow. For all of the grace and blessings, the world was still a tumultuous place.

Yes, there were still good people in it but there were also bad ones. John Thomas Rourke was a good one, the best I had met. But now, I could see the man behind what would one day be a legend. I could see his pain, the terrible senses of loss he felt. Yes, I said senses... the loss of his family, the loss of his world, the loss of innocence. Yet, each day he continued. My hope was one day he could find his own brand of peace in some valley.

EPILOGUE

This has been as accurate a first person account of what occurred to me during these early days with John Thomas Rourke and the events unfolding in our new world after the Russian attack, as I am capable of. However, there were a multitude of things happening that I did not have the opportunity to see, hear, or get briefed on in a timely fashion. I want to try and give you, my reader, the development and not the end result of this phase of our journey. Admittedly, looking back is proving far more difficult than I imagined. Sometimes it is difficult, if not impossible, to accurately relate where I was so long ago.

Dickens said in *The Tale of Two Cities*, "It was the best of times, it was the worst of times." This was true of our stories. It is strange that my research has shown me one thing in blinding clarity. I have changed more than I realized. Going back into the journey has reminded me of when I discovered certain truths, thoughts, and ideas that frankly I thought were just me, the ways I thought and felt. This exercise took me back down the roads and trails where I was learning to be the person I am today. It has been rather humbling to remember the "WHO" I was.

Much of my transformation is hard to discern as it developed from who I was then and who I am now. Jerry's stories tell you a far more complete account than I can offer. Remember this—I was living it at the time, at those moments, in the heat of turmoil and battle and, in this volume, at the end of my world. Much of whom I became I did not seek; in fact, I would not have wanted to be who I am today—not given the costs. But know this: I am glad I am who I am.

I was, I am, Everyman. Few people could ever become or would even want to be John Thomas Rourke. But, I am living proof that everyman can be better, stronger, and more self-reliant. I became a better man mostly because of John. To express my feelings about that process and to the man most responsible for that process, I must offer apologies to the Founders of America. I became a better husband and a better father because I held, or more accurately now hold, these "truths to be self-evident."

John told me a parable once about the lowly pencil. The Pencil Maker took the pencil aside, just before putting him into the box. "There are five things you need to know, he told the pencil, before I send you out into the world. Always remember them and never forget, and you will become the best pencil you can be."

"First of all, you will be able to do many great things, but only if you allow yourself to be held in someone's hand. Second, you will experience a painful sharpening from time to time, but you'll need it to become a better pencil. Third, you will be able to correct any mistakes you might make; thanks to the eraser I've given you. Fourth, remember the most important part of you will always be what's inside. And lastly, on every surface you are used on, you must leave your mark. No matter what the condition, you must continue to write."

The pencil understood and promised to remember, and went into the box with purpose in its heart. John then replaced the pencil with me and said if I always remember these and never forget, I would become the best person I could be.

He also told me about an essay he had come across a long time ago, written by a retired U.S. Army Lieutenant Colonel name Dave Grossman. It was called, *On Sheep, Wolves, and Sheepdogs*. John said it mirrored his life and has come to mirror my own.

It goes something like this. There are basically three groups of people in the world. The masses behave more like sheep. The sheepdogs come next and then there are the wolves. Grossman said, "The sheep generally do not like the sheepdog. He looks a lot like the wolf. He has fangs and the capacity for violence. The difference though, is that the sheepdog must not, cannot, and will not ever harm the sheep. Any sheepdog that intentionally harms the lowliest little lamb will be punished and removed. The world cannot work any other way, at least not in a representative democracy or a republic such as ours."

"But the sheep do not like the sheepdog; he is a constant reminder that there are wolves in the land. They would prefer that he didn't tell them where to go, or give them traffic tickets, or stand at the ready in our airports in camouflage fatigues holding an M-16. The sheep would much rather have the sheepdog cash in his fangs, spray paint himself white and go, 'Baa.'"

"Until the wolf shows up. Then the entire flock tries desperately to hide behind one lonely sheepdog. Understand that there is nothing morally superior about being a sheepdog; it is just what you choose to be. Also understand that a sheepdog is a funny critter: He is always sniffing around out on the perimeter, checking the breeze, barking at things that go bump in the night, and yearning for a righteous battle. That is the young sheepdogs yearn for a righteous battle. The old sheepdogs are a little older and wiser, but they move to the sound of the guns when needed right along with the young ones."

John Thomas Rourke was a sheepdog when I met him; he had made that choice long before that meeting. He went further and refined both the knowledge and skills necessary to be effective. It seems this business of being a sheep or a sheepdog is not a yes-no dichotomy. It is not an all-or-nothing, either-or choice. It is a matter of degrees, a continuum. On one end is an abject, head-in-the-sand-sheep and on the other end is the ultimate warrior. Few people exist completely on one end or the other. Most of us live somewhere in between. The sheep took a few steps toward accepting and appreciating their warriors and the warriors started taking their job more seriously. The degree to which you move up that continuum, away from sheep-hood and denial, is the degree to which you and your loved ones will survive, physically and psychologically at your moment of truth.

I think everyman comes to a place where he must grow or die; where he must become who he can be or remain who he was. I know that was true for me, I believe it was; it could be true for you. You see I learned that I was a "puppy" that had been raised as a sheep. I was a sheepdog; I just didn't know it. I had been raised with the sheep; I thought I was a sheep and I would have remained one. I didn't have that choice. I was faced with something I could not understand and had no training to deal with. But, I was also faced with the following choices:

1. Live or Die
2. Learn or Die
3. Improve or Die

John showed me the difference between a wolf and a sheepdog. Oh, and yes, I had a teacher that believed in me. I decided to live, learn, and improve because I didn't want to die. I said earlier "mostly because" of Rourke. I learned that part of the credit goes to me. I learned... I listened... I survived. Everyman has those opportunities at some time in his life. I took advantage of what was offered; therefore... so can you, if you chose to.

I think now you are ready for the next phase of our stories. This was the beginnings of the deeper aspects of my own transformation. Like you, I was "every man"; I was becoming Everyman... not a super hero by any means. But I did become a better man.

Our adventures, our journey... our quest, still has many twists and turns ahead. John told me once, "You have to be careful going down rabbit trails. A lot of the time all you find are skunks."

As bad as these early days were, I learned and grew. We found some beauty, some strength and peace, but we also found those skunks, ours were the two legged kind. Take your pick: cannibals, maniacs, traitors. This is just the first volume, there is more to come, so plan ahead.

For a complete story of the activities that began that day for me in the desert, find Jerry's original series. According to John Thomas Rourke, it is the most complete. If you choose to just focus on the history books, remember what Napoleon said, "History is nothing but an agreed upon set of lies."

*****

What else was happening while my part of the adventure was unfolding? These are some of the missing parts I did not see or did not hear myself. Things that I wouldn't even be aware of until much later. Those of you familiar with our story will think these tidbits are common knowledge. You need to understand, the final chapters of the world and the Rourke family had not be written yet. I want you to understand where we were, what we were dealing with and what we learned at the time.

"At the time." What a totally inadequate phrase that really was. Time had lost all meaning for us. It was simply measured by miles traveled, hardships overcome, disappointments we faced, and battles we survived. Remember, I wasn't writing this book at the time. I was immersed in what was happening. There was much we didn't know, had we known some of these things... Frankly, I don't know if it would have been better for us or worse. It simply ended up being the way it was. So, I will draw this tale to closure for you.

Sarah, Michael, and Annie: Sarah was already experiencing issues with John before this adventure began; the marriage had some difficulties. When John and I met after the plane crash, her world had already starting to spiral out of control. She and the children had survived the initial bombs only to be thrust into the nightmare world created by them. She was on her own search for John.

Natalia: Beautiful, deadly, and the most complicated woman I ever met. I fell in love with her during this episode and love her more today. I remember a line from John Greenleaf Whittier, "For of all sad words of tongue or pen, the saddest are these—it might have been." It would be a long time before Paul Rubenstein grew up. I would have never made it without her influence.

When I lost Ruth, my girlfriend, a part of me shut down. I knew she had died, I hoped it was not a painful and scary death. Natalia showed me that the part of me that died with Ruth was not totally dead, there was an ember left. Within the darkness there was a small, weak—almost, but not totally extinguished part of me that lived, still. I found I loved Natalia, at least from afar. It was a complicated situation, loving Natalia, loving John Thomas—wanting them to be together. Wanting her for myself. I can't explain it any better; I am glad she was and is in my life.

America: She was changed forever. Florida was gone, California was gone, and Reno, Nevada was beachfront property. Where there had been fertile plains and forests, now radioactive deserts stood. Russians had landed, one president was dead, and another was trying to save not only himself but the country; and yes, humanity—if it was possible. These were the darkest times in man's history and they weren't over.

None of us, or anyone else for that matter, had any idea if long term survival was possible. We were in the minute; in the second. Wrestling with the "time clock" for every moment of life we could squeeze out.

The underlying questions: Would America survive? Would we survive? Were we sure we even wanted to?

John Thomas Rourke: John became my mentor, my teacher, my friend, and my brother. I had never known and never will know anyone like John. John had prepared all of his adult life for this contingency, but it held dangers and complications he never imagined. It would still take a while for us to realize how much the world had changed.

191

Society as we knew it was over; paramilitary groups and armed bands of brigands existed, struggling for control—even though they had no idea of what there was to control. Life was a day-to-day existence, and it could end at any second. There was, of course, the matter of the mysterious Eden Project; some type of international project.

We really didn't understand what it even was. We didn't know if was a Doom's Day device, or a way to save some people from the catastrophe that had been set in motion; a way to ensure the survival of the humanity's survival at all costs in the event of a global nuclear confrontation.

The Past: The past is never really how you remember it. Sometimes, you can glimpse something from the corner of your eye called a memory. Sometimes, the scent of it wafts by on a gentle breeze. Rarely, if ever, is it accurate. One thing is for sure, you can't go back. In our case, there was literally nothing left to go back to. At least nothing we could see at this stage.

The Future: We didn't even know if there was going to be a future. All we had was right now, which could be stripped away in the next heartbeat. We did not think in terms of years, well I didn't anyway. We thought in terms of minutes and days and miles. Miles to the next benchmark, the next spot on the map, the next battle. The funny thing is someone said that, "You are never more alive than when you are about to die." It is true. God help me, but this was really the best time of my life. I finally understood what Confederate General, Robert E. Lee meant when he said, "It is good that war is so horrible, or we might grow to like it."

The Present: I heard a saying once, "Yesterday is history, tomorrow is a mystery, today is a gift of God; which is why we call it the present." I couldn't really see that our "today" was a gift; it was more like a sentence that had been imposed. I didn't feel it was from God either, but I couldn't truly blame it on Satan. This had been a gift we—man—had given to ourselves. How senseless, how foolish.

But for the moment, we were alive... so we must live. After all, what other choice do we have? It will be a long time before our questions had answers, before our quest would be finished. Finished, at the time of these events, I hoped one day it actually would be finished. How little we know sometimes.

Remember, this story is just beginning...

Made in the USA
Monee, IL
22 January 2021

58441958R00121